Making Peace

Where There's No Love

DEBORAH COOK

This is a work of fiction. Names, characters, places and incidents either are the product of the author's imagination or are used fictitiously, and any resemblance to actual persons, living or dead, business establishments, events, or locales is entirely coincidental.

ISBN: 978-0-9836767-1-3

Cover photograph © Simone Boynton

www.glidingpen.com

ACKNOWLEDGEMENTS

I'd like to thank with all my heart my little California family: Jonathan, Adrienne, Jovan, Sandra and Simone. They encouraged me throughout my writing process to continue writing and never give up. They were my editors, reviewers, supporters and critics. (Eden was born too late to be included here.)

A special thanks to my very dear friends Debbie Thompson, Jessie Hsieh, Maria Trejo, Mamie Wong, Mike Frias and Mark Oyama, who were there for me during my entire writing process. They did not give up on me during my dry spells, but continued to cheer me on to complete the novel.

I also want to thank Mitch Karno, Ph.D., a former boss, who gave me convincing words of encouragement. He displayed sincere confidence in my writing ability and assured me that I could and should write a novel.

And it is with deep gratitude that I also want to thank Joan for sharing valuable information with me on art and the operations of an art gallery. If any terminology or procedure in the novel is incorrect, I take full responsibility for the error(s).

Chapter One

Thump! Thump! Thump! . . . Thump! Thump! Thump! . . . Thump! Thump! Thump! Silence. It was late—11:00, to be exact, and they were standing on her porch, in the dark, banging on her door. She had a doorbell and door knocker they could have used, but they chose to bang on her door—repeatedly. Karen had gotten real cozy in her bed and was just about to go into a deep, satisfying sleep when they started up with the banging. They didn't call out and announce who it was, but she knew: it was her siblings.

They had called her on the phone, one by one, several times, and she refused to answer. That's the advantage of having caller ID: you know in advance who's calling, then you can avoid the agony of trying to end a conversation with someone you didn't want to talk to in the first place. They blocked their numbers on the phone, and she still would not pick up; she never answered blocked calls.

They left messages; she ignored them. She did not return their calls then, and had no intention of ever calling them in the future. Karen had distanced herself from them a while back, and she wanted it to stay that way—forever.

"Mom is in the hospital. She had a heart attack. She isn't expected to make it past the weekend," was Helen's message on the answering machine. Helen was the eldest sibling. There were four of them: three girls and a boy.

Helen usually was the one in charge, the spokesperson. She didn't wait to be nominated; she would take the lead and the others always fell in line. This time, the others had designated her to make the first call, and she did. But if they hadn't asked her, she would have volunteered anyway. It didn't take much effort to convince Helen to take action.

The others thought Karen would surely respond to Helen, but they were wrong, because she didn't, and when she didn't respond to Helen's call, the other two took turns calling. They called in the morning before Karen left the house for work, in the afternoon, although they figured she wouldn't be there, because she usually wasn't at that time, and again in the evening, because they were sure she'd be there.

No matter when they called, they couldn't catch her. They had hoped Karen would answer or return one of their calls, but she didn't. This was their last resort—going to her house, in person, and bang on her door. They were not to be ignored.

Karen's first thought was to do just that: ignore them, and hope they'd give up and go away. It was obvious that they didn't care if she was asleep or not. Otherwise, they would have gone earlier in the evening.

Maybe they would think she wasn't home, and leave, she thought. But then again, she knew, realistically, that Helen was relentless; she'd never give up. And, of course, the others would follow suit. If necessary, they would camp out all night on her porch, despite the chilly, fall, Los Angeles-area night air. Karen's car was in the driveway; that was a strong indication that she was at home. And, when it came right down to it, they knew she was home; she usually was in the evening.

To avoid having them disturb her neighbors any further with their incessant banging, Karen dragged herself out of bed, grabbed her robe, which was draped over the bedpost, threw it on and headed to the door.

"Who is it?" she called out on her way to the door, as if she didn't know.

"It's us, Karen! You know who it is." It was Helen answering, of course, doing her spokesperson duty. Karen turned on her porch light when she reached the door and peeked through the peephole as if to confirm it was actually them.

There they were: Helen and Brigit were in front and Daniel was just behind them. Three pairs of blue eyes focused on the door, unflinching, despite the glare of her porch light nearly blinding them.

Karen unlocked the door, slowly opened it and stepped in the doorway to block them from entering—just in case they tried. She had no intention of letting them in. They could have their say while on the porch, and leave.

"Yes?" she questioned, as though she were clueless as to why they would get together and travel to her house late at night. They didn't live a long distance away; the three lived within fifteen minutes of each other, and about a half hour away from Karen. Helen lived in Santa Monica, CA; Brigit, Westwood, CA; and Danny, West Los Angeles, CA, while Karen, on the other hand, lived in West Hollywood, CA. Danny and Helen met up at Brigit's house, and Danny drove all three to Karen's. So, while it wasn't far, it was late, and they did have to travel to get to her.

"We need to talk to you—inside. Are you going to let us in, or do you intend to keep us out here on the porch?" Helen demanded. Helen crossed her arms and exchanged a quick look with Brigit. Daniel stood silent, staring into Karen's eyes. Getting rid of them wasn't going to be easy.

Karen took a deep breath and weighed her options: She could argue with them while on her porch or let them in. Arguing could prolong their presence on her porch, and they might refuse to have their say unless allowed inside. Letting them in would entail listening to what they had to say, and having them in her house, but maybe they would have their say and leave quickly. She could only hope. She decided to let them in.

She stepped behind the door, opened it a little wider, and allowed them to enter. There was no exchange of affection as they entered. They didn't hug or kiss as a lot of families do; they weren't like that—at least not with Karen.

Karen didn't feel close to any of her siblings. While the others were close to each other, they were not close to her. Karen had come to accept that, and she used that as part of her reason for completely distancing herself from them. At this point, her siblings were no longer a part of her life.

"You're in, so what do you want?" Karen asked immediately after Daniel entered, just behind the girls.

"First of all, to sit down," Helen said.

"Why? You're inside. Why don't you say what you have to say, and then you can leave?" The three pairs of eyes stared at Karen. No one said a word. She waited. Silence. They weren't backing down. Karen sighed. She motioned for them to go into the living room. They walked into the room without uttering a word to each other, or her, and sat down on the sofa. Karen continued standing.

"We left you messages that mom is in the hospital, and we haven't heard back from you," Helen said. A look of desperation took over Helen's face. Karen studied the bags Helen had under her puffy, murky eyes. It seemed as though she were struggling to keep them opened; she looked exhausted.

Karen had never seen Helen like that before. And Helen usually spoke with confidence and authority; people listened to her. But her voice lacked its usual demand for compliance. And usually the model of perfection, with everything in place, Helen's blouse and slacks being wrinkled, her makeup uneven, and her short, tapered hair clinging to her scalp were all out of character.

"She's dying, Karen," Helen continued.

"And . . ?" Karen replied as she shrugged her shoulders. The group looked at Karen in disbelief: their eyes widened and their mouths flew open. They all knew Karen had distanced herself from their mother too, but they never imagined that she could be so heartless—that she didn't even care about her mother's well-being.

Brigit thought that maybe Karen didn't realize the gravity of the situation. Brigit gave everyone the benefit of a doubt, and she didn't want to deny Karen of the same opportunity—the opportunity to redeem herself.

"You may never get a chance to see her alive again," Brigit blurted out. "You should go to see her now." Brigit waited for a sign of remorse and some indication that Karen was moved by this news.

"What benefit is there in seeing someone just before they die?" Karen asked. "What is the purpose? What will it accomplish? I haven't seen her in over a year." She opened her eyes as wide as she could, shrugged, and waited for an answer. No answer. She eyed the group and waited.

"If nothing else, you can make peace," Danny jumped in. "She's your mother, Karen. She deserves at least a last visit from you. You owe it to her, if for no other reason than . . . than having you." Danny gave Karen a 'you should be ashamed of yourself' look and then stared at her starting from her eyes, which he locked with his own, and worked his way all the way down to her ankles and back up to her eyes.

He loved his mother; he was her favorite child. The others knew and accepted that. Danny was incensed that Karen could be so insensitive to their mother's impending death. They all looked at Karen and waited for her to respond.

Karen felt tears well in her eyes. She couldn't determine if it was anger or a slight pang of conscience. Whatever it was, it was unpleasant. They were staring at her the way jurors do when they pronounce sentence on a criminal.

She became incensed. How dare they come to her house and judge her. She wanted to explode and put them in their place, tell them what she thought of them. Instead, she lowered her head, chewed at the inside of her bottom lip and looked away; she said nothing.

"Well?" Brigit continued. "Are you going to go?" Brigit used a tone that was more of a plea than an order. That was Brigit's tactic: rather than demand, she tried to appeal to people. Karen didn't answer. "Please go, Karen. You don't have to stay long—maybe 10 minutes." Karen raised her head and faced them. She stared at the three and still said nothing.

"We're begging you," Brigit pleaded. Brigit cupped her hands together as if praying and held them close to her chest. Karen stared at Brigit's display of emotion. Though unaffected, Karen felt trapped. There were three of them against only one of her, and they were in her house. She wanted them out. She regretted having let them in and allowing them to sit down. Now she had the task of getting them out.

"Okay . . . Okay, I'll go," Karen said, her voice barely audible. I don't see what good it will do, but I'll go." She looked at each one square in the face. "Satisfied?" she asked.

They nodded in unison but didn't say a word. They knew

when to shut up. This was one of those times. Any further comments could cause Karen to change her mind, and they didn't want to risk it. Although Karen didn't see the importance of visiting their mother, they did; it was important to them. They decided to leave immediately.

They gave each other a quick look. They stood up and proceeded toward the door. When they approached the door, Brigit paused, turned, and looked at Karen.

"One of us will be there when you go. We've been taking turns staying with her. Aunt Pam's there now, and I'm on my way. So . . . we'll see you later," Brigit said. Brigit waited for confirmation; none was given. "Good-bye, Karen," said Brigit.

The others gave Karen a good-bye nod as they stepped through the doorway. She gave them a blank stare. Karen closed the door behind them and leaned back on it. She took a deep breath and held it until she had no choice but to release it and take in another one.

Karen had a difficult time trying to sleep that night. She couldn't get comfortable no matter how she fluffed her pillows or positioned her body on the bed. And she suffered with what she considered to be the worst headache of her life. She often suffered with headaches when she had to make important decisions: buying a house, a car, opening her own business, and at that time, going to visit her dying mother. The other headaches seemed mild compared to the one she had at that time.

Thoughts continued to race through her mind about her siblings—the whole ordeal. Her mind wouldn't rest, and it wouldn't allow her body to rest. She was going against her will "to make peace," as they called it, with her mother, and she resented it. That night seemed endless.

Chapter Two

The next day, Karen put the visit to her mother off until evening. She didn't want to go early and have the visit ruin her entire day; besides, she had things to do. It was Sunday. Although she believed in God, and that he existed, she wasn't accustomed to going to church, so that didn't take up any of her time. But there was always housecleaning, grocery shopping and washing clothes to keep her busy—anything to put off visiting her mother for as long as possible. She did them all, and looked for other home chores she had neglected.

When evening approached, Karen figured she couldn't put the visit off any longer. None of her siblings had called to say her mother had died, so she had to assume that she was still breathing.

Karen finally convinced herself to make the trip to the hospital and get it over with. She had said she was going to go, and she was good at keeping her word. And she didn't want another late-night visit because she did not go.

The antiseptic/anti-bacterial odor in the hospital smelled more like death than life to Karen. It settled in the back of her throat; it tasted horrible. She stopped at a nearby water fountain to try to rinse it out of her mouth and throat. She gulped some water and swallowed hard. The water and bad taste dropped into her stomach. They made her sick to her stomach, but she decided to cope with it.

She looked around at the expressionless faces of people sitting, standing and walking. To her, they looked more like zombies awaiting their fate rather than visitors to cheer up the sick with words of hope. It was a sad, sick-smelling place. Karen went to the information desk to get a visitor's pass.

"I'm here to see Frances Andersen," Karen said. The security guard behind the desk found Frances' name on the hospital list and informed her that only immediate family was allowed. "I'm her daughter," Karen said. She leaned in. "At least that's what I was told." She raised an eyebrow and smirked.

The guard didn't find her comment amusing. Straight faced, he also raised an eyebrow, asked for ID and provided her with the pass. He directed her to the nurse's station on the third floor. She stuffed herself in the elevator with a bunch of zombie-looking people and got off on the third floor.

"She's in room 3140. It's that way, at the end of the hall," one of the nurses said as she pointed down a long hallway. Karen followed the nurse's direction.

On her way, she stopped to view every single piece of art displayed on the walls of the long corridor, taking time to carefully analyze each one. To the average person, there wasn't much to analyze: they seemed to be ordinary paintings of gardens and countrysides. For hospital staff, and most visitors, their purpose was to cover up barren walls and provide some color, which they did, but for Karen, they had more to offer.

She carefully studied each painting's color, light, balance, etc. She lingered at each painting for a long while, then moved on to the next one. Eventually, she reached her dreaded destination: her mother's hospital room.

As she entered her mother's room, Karen was shocked to see all of her siblings there. Brigit had said they were taking turns, but all of them were there, along with her Aunt Pamela. Pamela was her mother's sister and Karen's favorite aunt—she had two. Her other aunt was on her dad's side of the family. She was the wife of her dad's only brother. They moved to Florida when Karen was in grade school, and Karen hadn't gotten as close to her as she had to Pamela.

Pamela rushed over to Karen and held her tight. Overwhelmed, Karen lost her breath. She gasped; her heart pounded hard and fast.

"We're losing her," Pamela said. She squeezed Karen tighter. "We're gonna lose Frannie. We're losing your mom.

We've got to be strong." Pamela's eyes welled with tears. The others looked on, waiting for a response from Karen.

As far as Karen was concerned, whether her mother lived or died, meant nothing to her. She didn't have any feelings for her mother and she wasn't going to act as though she did. Karen prided herself with being an upfront person. She sighed and loosened Pamela's grip.

"I know," Karen said. "And I'm here to say good-bye," she said with very little emotion, as if she were reading lines she was unable to memorize. Tears trickled down Pamela's face, and she sniffled. Unaffected, Karen turned to face the others and stared at them. They gave her their full attention. They waited for her words of grief or remorse.

"I'm here to say good-bye to my mother, or what you all call 'to make peace,'" she said to the group. She stared at them, one by one. She made an air quote with the words "to make peace" to make it clear that it was their term and not hers. "Can I do it alone, or do I have to have all of you standing around, looking on? I think I'm entitled to some privacy."

They looked at each other and gave her a nod. Helen shrugged her shoulders and sighed. She tilted her head in the direction of the door, signaling the others to follow her as she headed for it. They followed.

"We'll be outside," Helen said as they left the room.

Karen watched as the door closed behind them. She strolled over to her mother's bedside, stood there for a long time, just staring at her, before saying anything.

Her mother was unconscious. There was no movement to indicate that she was aware of Karen's presence. She had numerous tubes and wires connecting her to machinery and monitors. Karen's eyes followed the length of some of the tubes from her mother to the machines they belonged to, then from the wires to their monitors.

She thought to herself how weak and helpless her mother looked as she lay there. Karen almost felt sorry for her mother, but dismissed that feeling.

Her mother looked nothing like the exuberant older woman she remembered from the last time she had seen her. Instead,

Karen thought her mother looked more like a medical experiment or alien rather than a human: her eyes, though closed, looked sunken in with dark, wrinkled circles around them, her complexion looked pale and pasty, and she was so thin she looked emaciated. And her lips had a white chalky substance on them that made them look dry and cracked.

Karen leaned over, got close to her mother's ear and whispered, "Well . . . I'm here to say good-bye. It's me, Karen, the one you didn't have time for. Remember me? You know, the one that just couldn't do anything right. Nothing I did pleased you, mother, and I finally accepted that I would never be able to please you. Humph! And you know what? I'm not really here for you. The others sent me to make peace with you . . ."

Karen took a deep breath and got even closer to her mother's face. She could feel her own hot breath bounce off her mother's face onto hers as she exhaled. She studied her mother's face one last time.

"There will never be peace between us, mother. Only good-bye. So . . . good-bye." With that said, Karen felt a touch of emotion coming on. She quickly turned away, first her head, then her entire body. Karen had taught herself to hide her feelings—especially from her mother. The fact that her mother was half dead didn't change anything.

She did not turn around again or look back to take one last glimpse of her mother. Instead, Karen then left her mother's bedside. In her haste to make a fast exit, Karen did not notice a slight quiver of her mother's right eye.

The others were busy in conversation when Karen left her mother's room and entered the hallway. They stopped. They stared at her, and she at them.

"I'm through. I came as you asked, and I'm done," Karen said to the group. The look she gave them dared them to ask any questions or to start a conversation.

"Thank you," Brigit said. "We'll keep in touch and let you know when it happens." She knew what "it" meant; no explanation was necessary. She nodded. Pam grabbed Karen again and kissed her. "We've got to re-connect. Okay?"

"Yes, Aunt Pammy. I'll give you a call," Karen said. And she meant it. She hugged her aunt, nodded at the others and left. Karen and her Aunt Pamela used to be very close. As far as Karen was concerned, they were more like mother and daughter than aunt and niece.

Karen used to spend some weekends over Pamela's house. They'd go shopping together, and just hang out; they always had a good time. And since Pam didn't have any girls of her own, there wasn't any competition for attention. Karen had her all to herself. Pam's boys would be off with their dad, and Pam would be with Karen.

But with time and college, their phone calls became hit and miss, and eventually, the only time they saw each other were at family gatherings—which Karen avoided. They drifted apart, and gradually lost touch altogether. They hadn't seen each other in over a year. Seeing her aunt again brought back memories.

Several days passed before Karen heard from her siblings with any news about their mother. She was busy in the kitchen washing dishes when she got the call. It was Brigit.

"We didn't call you earlier," Brigit said, "because mom made a turnaround."

"Turnaround? What do you mean turnaround?" Karen's voice resounded with definite surprise but lacked in enthusiasm.

"I mean that she's improving. They're giving her a 50-50 chance that she'll survive. Isn't that great?" Karen didn't share Brigit's enthusiasm. Karen found the information perplexing. She wondered how it could be possible that their mother was improving, when she was close to death when she saw her.

She grabbed a nearby chair and sat down with the phone next to her ear; she drifted in thought. She wondered the extent of improvement: stronger vital signs, eye movement or muscle twitching, but didn't ask. She said nothing. She then heard Brigit calling out.

"Are you there? Karen . . . hello . . . are you there?" Brigit's voice startled her and abruptly brought her back to reality.

"Yes . . . I'm here," Karen growled. "I . . . I just don't know what to say."

"You could say you're happy that our mother has a chance of surviving," Brigit said, her voice shaking. Brigit held back her tears and tried to remain calm. "That's what you could say, Karen." Karen gave a sigh that resonated over the phone.

"Thanks for calling, Brigit, and let me know what happens, okay?"

"Sure, I'll call you, but you should stop by and visit her again," Brigit pleaded. She paused to allow time for Karen to respond. She didn't. After a long pause, Brigit gave up waiting. Brigit thought it best to terminate the call, because she felt herself becoming angry; it was an emotion she tried very hard to avoid.

"I'll talk to you later," Brigit said. "Good-bye, Karen." Karen hung up the phone. She sat, frozen: dazed by the news. She had already visited her mother once at their insistence; she was not going to allow them to force her to do it again. She decided that no matter what tactic they used, she wasn't going to give in this time. She did not return to the hospital or call for an update on her mother's health. She waited.

Several days passed without hearing any information about her mother. Neither Karen's siblings nor her Aunt Pam called her. The suspense was killing Karen. Maybe they forgot to call her, she thought. But how could they? They couldn't possibly bury their mother without her being present, she thought. She had to know what was happening. She called Brigit but only got her answering machine. She left a message.

"Brigit, this is Karen. You were supposed to call me with an update. I'm waiting." Brigit didn't return her call. Instead, there was another late-night visit.

"And what's the problem now?" Karen asked the group as they stood on the porch. They remained silent, staring at her, until Karen opened the door and allowed them to enter. They went inside. Karen led the way for them to follow her to the living room. After a few steps, she noticed that they had not moved; they remained just inside the door. She turned to face them.

"Brigit asked you to visit mom, and you didn't," Helen said, as she tried to control her anger.

"And how do you know? You don't know that for sure."

"Know what? That Brigit asked you to go, or that you didn't visit?"

"How do you know whether or not I visited?" Karen thought

she'd give the impression that she had visited when they weren't there. How could they possibly know for sure unless they checked with security and checked the sign-in sheets? She doubted they did that. She concluded that they were assuming she hadn't visited, and didn't know for sure. The burden of proof was on them, and she wasn't about to back down. She crossed her arms and waited for an answer.

"Because mom said you didn't come," Helen said as she crossed her arms too.

"Mother said that? What are you saying? That she can talk?" Karen thought that her mother's vital signs may have improved a little, but that she was still unconscious. She didn't think that her improvement was to the point of being able to speak or recognize faces of people visiting her. She was snagged.

"Yes, and you'd know that if you had visited," Brigit yelled. Brigit temporarily lost her tactic of appealing to someone with kindness. She caught herself and immediately calmed down. She slid her hands along the sleeves of her jacket as if to smooth out any wrinkles and gave Karen a half smile.

"She seems to be coming along fine. She's very weak though, and if everything goes well, it's possible she'll be released in a few weeks, Helen added. Helen dropped her arms and clasped her hands in front. "We're going to need you to pitch in and help, Karen," she said.

"And she's been asking for you," Brigit blurted out.

"Me? She asked for me?" Karen asked in disbelief. She wondered why her mother would ask for her when they hadn't communicated in over a year. Karen thought that having her other precious children there with her should have been good enough.

Silent until then, Danny shuffled over to Karen and whispered, "She's *your* mother too. And you should remember that." Danny pushed the wrong button. Karen shook her head.

"You're wrong, little brother. Remember . . ? I know she's my mother. SHE'S the one you should remind," Karen screamed. Danny threw his hands up and sighed; Brigit rolled her eyes. Helen, on the other hand, ignored Karen's outburst and continued where she had left off, before the others interjected their comments. She restrained herself from raising her voice.

"Then, can we count on you?" Helen asked. "If everything goes well, she's going to stay with me. We're going to have a nurse part-time to help out during the week, and if you could help out a couple of hours on the weekend, I'd really appreciate it." Helen looked at Brigit and Danny, then back at Karen. "We all would," Helen continued.

Helen then reached out and placed her hand toward the front of Karen's shoulder. The hand placement was not a sign of affection, but a way to keep Karen's focus and attention on what she was saying. To Karen, though, Helen's hand was like dead weight, and it was becoming heavier by the second. Karen didn't answer; instead, she stared at Helen's hand that was touching her. Helen got the message. She immediately moved her hand off Karen and dropped it to her side.

"Thank you," Helen said despite not having received any form of commitment from Karen. "We'll let you know when she's released."

"IF she's released," Karen said just above a whisper as they exited. She raised her eyebrows and repeated a little louder, so they could hear, "IF . . ."

Frances' health did improve. Within a month, she was released from the hospital and taken to Helen's home. Prior to that, no one heard from Karen. Karen thought that if she didn't keep in touch with them, they would forget about including her in their mother-care plans. She hoped they would recognize her absence as a sign of disinterest. But she was wrong: her siblings didn't care about how she felt—or they were still in denial, refusing to accept that Karen didn't care about their mother's well-being.

Karen was drafted to assist with her mother's care a couple of hours a week. It was a task Karen didn't want to take on, but she figured it wouldn't last too long: either her mother would die or get better—Karen didn't care which one—then her services would no longer be needed. And then she wouldn't have to have any further contact with her siblings. She looked forward to that.

Chapter Three

Helen led Karen to the living room. It was Karen's first turn at helping out with her mother's care; Frances had been released from the hospital six weeks earlier. For the first month, they had a full-time nurse during the week to care for her. They now had a part-time nurse stop by a couple of afternoons during the week to assist her, because Frances had improved greatly, to the point where she was mobile and doing many things on her own.

Frances was sitting on the sofa watching TV as they walked in. Karen and Frances stared at each other and didn't say a word. Besides the obvious—that she was conscious—Karen thought Frances looked a lot better than when she was in the hospital: she had gained weight and filled in a little, and her skin had gotten some color. Semi-closed, her eyes looked weak and tired, but the big smile she gave Karen erased any hint of that. She opened her eyes wide so that they smiled too.

"Karen . . . I'm glad you came," Frances said. She reached out her still frail arms for Karen to embrace her. Karen walked over to her and gave her a half smile. She bent down, touched the side of her mother's face with her own, and lightly patted her on the back. Frances gave Karen a light hug.

"Hello, mother . . . I guess I'm here to help you out." Karen looked over at Helen. "Helen apparently has family plans," Karen said.

"Yes, Josh has a little league game this afternoon; we're all going," Helen confirmed. Brad, Helen's husband entered the room with their two boys. Towering over Karen, Brad tapped her shoulder. At 6'4", Brad towered over the average person. He had played high school and college football—and was good at it. He still looked like a quarterback, but with a few extra pounds put on.

"Good to see you, Kar. Thanks for coming," Brad said. Karen gave him a nod. Deep down, she liked Brad. He was an easy-going and likeable type, the type of man other men looked up to and wanted to have as a buddy. The boys looked back and forth from Helen to Karen. They weren't sure as to how they should react toward Karen: how they should treat her. They knew who Karen was, but they hadn't seen her in a long time.

"Boys, aren't you going to hug your Aunt Karen?" Helen asked. The boys ran over to Karen, wrapped their arms around her and hugged her together. She patted them and stepped back to get a better look at them.

"You boys have gotten so big, I barely recognized you." Karen touched the top of their heads. "And you've gotten so tall. I bet you're gonna be tall just like your dad. How old are you guys?" she asked.

"I'm nine," Josh said, pointing to himself.

"And I'm six," Nicholas announced with pride as he hopped up and down. Karen looked at Helen and Brad, then at the boys. She gave a sheepish grin and shrugged her shoulders.

"I guess it has been a little while," Karen said. She gave the boys a second look over. "Well, go on to your ball game and have a good time." She smiled at Josh and shook her fists in the air. "And win! Okay, Josh?" Josh gave Karen a big grin and nodded with enthusiasm.

"Okay, gang, let's go," Brad said, clapping his hands. The boys raced over to Frances to kiss her before leaving with their parents. Once they left, it was then just Karen and Frances—alone. They stared at each other for a while, silent. Frances smiled.

"So, what do you want to do?" Frances asked, trying to break just one of the many boulders of ice separating them. Karen shrugged her shoulders and sat down on the sofa with Frances.

"I don't know. What do you need help with?" Karen figured she was supposed to help her eat, walk, or possibly hand her things that were too far for her to reach.

"Nothing. I think you're supposed to just keep me company. Do you want to talk? We can do that, Karen, if you want." Frances hoped they could spend some quality time together. She searched Karen's face and implored her with her eyes.

"Talk about what?" Karen asked. Karen looked away. She wondered what they could possibly have in common to talk about. She really didn't know much about her mother. To Karen, her mother was a mother in title only: she gave birth to her. She was a mother to her estranged siblings: she took an interest in them and cared for them. But to Karen, she and her mother were like strangers—and as far as she was concerned, they could remain that way. Karen was just fulfilling a duty imposed on her by her siblings—nothing more.

"I don't know. Anything. How about you: your health, the house, car, or . . . maybe the gallery?"

"The gallery?" Karen repeated. She looked into her mother's eyes to determine if her mother was truly interested, and whether or not her question deserved a detailed answer. She didn't dwell on it too long: she decided it didn't. Her mother may have been sincerely interested in the gallery, but Karen didn't want to share.

"It's going fine," Karen replied. She scanned the sofa table for the TV remote. Spying it, she reached over, picked it up, raised it in the air and waved it back and forth. "Why don't we watch TV? I'm sure they don't want you to exert yourself too much, and talking might be too exhausting for you."

She thought to herself that even if it wasn't too much for her mother, it would be too much for her, and would probably be emotionally draining. She didn't want to talk to her mother; she was doing the best she could just being in her presence.

Frances tried to convince Karen that having a conversation wouldn't require or expend much energy, but Karen wouldn't hear of it. Karen aimed the remote at the TV and turned it on. Frances was hurt, but tried not to show it. She gave a weak smile and turned toward the TV. She watched TV along with Karen. They sat together in silence. When one program ended, Karen found another one she figured both of them would enjoy, or tolerate, watching. She did not consult with Frances to see what she would be interested in seeing, or if she agreed with her selection. Time passed slowly for the two.

When Helen and her family returned, they found Frances sitting on the sofa where they had left her, but sound asleep. She had dozed off in front of the TV. Karen was sitting on the sofa flipping through channels searching for something new to watch. Frances awoke when she heard the noise from the door opening and closing and the boys running into the house.

"We won!" Josh shouted. "We won, grandma." He charged into the living room ahead of the others and hopped on the sofa next to Frances. The others entered the room.

"Good for you, Josh. I can't wait until I can go too and see you play," Frances said, still a little groggy. She hugged Josh and kissed his forehead.

"And how about you and Karen?" Helen asked. She then looked at Karen and directed her question to her. "Did you two enjoy yourselves?" Helen asked with forced enthusiasm. She stared at Karen and waited for a response. Karen returned the stare and refused to answer.

"Of course we did," Frances cut in. "We watched TV together." Surprised by her mother's statement, Karen glanced at Frances and gave way to a sheepish smile. Frances smiled at Karen. Helen's anger flared up. Her fake enthusiasm and smile she had painted on her face vanished in an instant. She was unable to restrain herself.

"That's it? You watched TV together?" Helen demanded. Helen looked at Karen, took a deep breath and exhaled to try to calm herself down. It was crystal clear that she was upset: her voice had gotten louder with each word and her eyes were on the verge of bulging out of their sockets.

Brad ordered the boys to go to their room, and he also fled from the area. Brad did not get involved in family matters between Helen and her siblings. The best way to avoid it at this time was to vacate the area. His decision making was limited to the Mitchell family. Here, he drew the line.

"That was fine, Helen, because we got a chance to spend some time together," Frances said, bubbling with joy. Helen shook her head in disgust. She looked at Karen, squinted her eyes at her, and walked away, leaving the room. Helen wanted to avoid further confrontation with Karen. She felt the only way to do that was by removing herself from Karen's presence, so she left.

"I guess I'd better go, then," Karen said to Frances. "I have to stop by the gallery for a bit. I'll see you tomorrow, mother. I'll let myself out." Frances nodded and smiled. Karen made a quick exit out the door without looking back.

Helen waited until she heard the door close, and then re-entered the room with Frances. She positioned herself in front of Frances, shook her head and began pacing back and forth.

"Mom, we don't need Karen's help. If she's going to come here and just watch TV, what's the purpose? It's not as though you're an infant who needs someone to sit with them. I say we tell her not to bother coming back."

"It's okay, honey. I'm happy she's willing to come at all. Please don't make a big deal out of it, okay?" Helen stopped in her tracks.

"A big deal?" Helen said with a lot of indignation. She studied her mother's face. Frances gave her a warm smile. Helen opened her hands, palms up, and extended them to Frances, pleading, without saying a word. She then shook her head again and sighed in resignation.

"Brigit said she's available, mom; we don't need Karen's help. But if that's what you want, it's up to you." Frances assured Helen that it was what she wanted. Helen had no alternative but to respect her mother's wish; she left the arrangement as it was.

* * *

It was a Saturday evening at Brigit's house. Brigit was hosting a family gathering. She was busy running around carrying food to the dinner table; Helen was helping. Frances, Helen, Brad and the boys, Daniel, Brigit's husband Michael, and their daughter Melissa were seated around the table, talking. Frances ended a conversation she was having with Melissa and looked around as if searching for something. Brigit and Helen entered the room with dishes of food in hand.

"Is Karen coming?" Frances asked the group, directing the question to no one in particular. No one answered. They continued with their conversations. Frances cleared her throat and spoke louder. "I asked if Karen is coming?" The men looked at each other, shrugged their shoulders, and then looked at Brigit. Karen didn't usually attend family gatherings, and she hadn't been to one in over a year. They didn't know the answer; maybe Brigit did. They looked at Brigit for the answer. Brigit put the dish of food down on the table and sighed. She shook her head.

"No, she's not coming, mom. Karen won't be here," Brigit answered.

"Did you invite her?"

"Helen did."

Frances looked at Helen for confirmation that she had invited Karen, and hopefully, an answer as to whether or not she'd be there. Although Brigit said with certainty that Karen wasn't going to be there, Frances hoped she was misinformed. Since Frances had already made it clear that she wanted Karen to be included in family gatherings, Helen felt insulted that Frances would even ask that question.

"Of course I invited her. She said she had to be at the gallery. Okay?" Helen barked. Helen put her dish down and walked away in a huff. Brigit scanned the table, giving it a once-over to see if any dish needed to be replenished.

"It looks like we need some more bread," she said as she followed Helen into the kitchen. Once in the kitchen, Brigit tried to calm Helen down, who was just about to reach her boiling point.

"It's okay," Brigit said as she approached Helen from behind. She patted Helen's shoulder, walked around to face her, and looked in Helen's eyes. "Calm down, Helen, it'll be okay." Helen clenched her fists and held them close to the side of her body.

"It makes me so angry that she keeps asking for Karen when we're the ones who are looking out for her."

"And she appreciates that, Helen, but, I guess, she would like Karen to be here too, so that it would be all of us. That's all." Helen nodded although she disagreed and failed to see the logic. Brigit continued to try to reason with Helen and to console her. Brigit's concern wasn't that Frances asked for Karen, but the reason as to why Karen refused to attend family functions. Brigit wondered why Karen alienated herself from everyone—including her.

"You didn't ask about Lauren. She's not here," Danny said to his mother in response to her asking about Karen. Lauren was Danny's girlfriend; they had recently started living together. They had been together for a couple of years and she frequently attended family gatherings. She was more a part of the family than Karen, and Danny wanted to make sure his mother recognized that. While Karen hadn't attended a family gathering in the past year, Lauren often did.

"Yes, I noticed Lauren isn't here, and although you two have been together for a long time, she still isn't family, Danny. And anyway, I'm asking about one of my own children. Surely, you can't find fault with that."

Immediately after her statement, Frances looked at Brad and Michael. Neither was offended by her comment, but Frances was afraid they may have taken it the wrong way, and she didn't want that. After all, they weren't her children by birth, and they were there—and she appreciated it. She loved them dearly; they called her 'mom.'

"Brad . . . Michael . . . I'm sorry; you know what I mean. You know that you're both like sons to me, and you . . . you are family." The men nodded and continued eating. They knew Frances loved them and had wholeheartedly embraced them as sons, so there wasn't any reason to complain or to get their feelings hurt over her statement—especially Michael. He was a handsome but very shy computer geek who was wholeheartedly, or according to him, overwhelmingly embraced by Frances and the entire family.

He and Brigit met on the job; he was one of the company's computer techs. At times, Brigit would see him on her floor working on people's computers, chatting with the users while doing so. Feeling left out, Brigit wanted to be included in his conversations too. Michael would have loved that too, but he was too shy to talk to her on his own.

Brigit tried to strike up conversations with him when he was in her work area, but their conversations ended up being short greetings. Dissatisfied with that, Brigit mysteriously started having computer problems that only he could fix, although another tech may have been available. After Michael responded to several service calls by Brigit, only to discover that her computer's problem would not occur in his presence so he could fix it, they too also were chatting.

The rest is history. They began dating and eventually got married. He was now a full-fledged member of the Andersen family. So dismissing Frances' comment was easy for Michael. He and Brad continued eating. Frances sighed.

"Maybe she'll make it next time," she whispered. No one made an effort to agree or disagree with her statement. Instead, they returned to their conversations.

Chapter Four

"Where's Uncle Scott?" Karen asked as she took a seat on the sofa in her Aunt Pamela's home. Pamela sat next to her.

"I'm not quite sure," Pamela answered. "He's hanging out with Chris and Ryan. I don't know where they went. I told him to get lost so we could have time to be by ourselves—some girl time. He loves hanging out with the boys anyway, so that gave him a good excuse to do it. I think he wishes they were still little boys living at home. You should go by and visit your cousins sometime. They don't live far from here. They ask about you."

Karen folded, then unfolded her arms, crossed her legs, and rhythmically bobbed her foot on the crossed leg. She didn't respond. She wasn't surprised that they had asked about her, because, after all, she used to spend a lot of time at their house, and she did feel close to them. Or at least she used to feel close to them.

She took a quick look at the room. She hadn't been there in a while; she noticed the furniture had been moved, and some new paintings had been added on the walls, as well as updated pictures of the boys. She smiled as she thought of the good times they had together.

"So . . . what are we going to do?" Karen asked.

"I'll leave that up to you," Pamela said. "We can go out for lunch nearby at the mall, or if you want, just stay here and hang around the house. I can fix us some sandwiches. I just bought some lunchmeat, and we always have canned tuna on hand. It's your choice."

"Let's stay here. Then we can talk. It doesn't matter what kind of sandwiches you fix; I'm open." Pamela loved that idea. She and Karen hadn't been together in a long time, and for Karen to want to talk about anything made her happy. Pamela missed the good times they had together, and so did Karen.

"Is there something in particular you want to talk about?" Pamela asked cautiously. Bringing up the wrong subject could prove disastrous and end the conversation before it began. If Karen suggested talking, Pamela figured Karen must have had something in mind she wanted to talk about. Pamela took the wise course by having Karen choose the topic. The question was, what was she willing to talk about?

"No, but we haven't had a chance to talk in a while, so we've got a lot of catching up to do," Karen said. She gave Pamela a warm smile.

"In that case: how's the gallery coming along?" Pam knew that the gallery was a safe topic and could act as an ice breaker. She was right. Karen was passionate about art and proud of her gallery. It showed on her face as her eyes lit up and a smile took over her entire face. She clasped her hands and raised them just below her chin.

"You should come by sometime. Compared to what people consider an average-size gallery, it's small—only 1200 square feet—so we have to make the most of our space. I had some partitions installed to give us some more display area, and we use it all. We carry mostly originals, with a few prints. Most of our artists are here in California. We have one who lives on the east coast, because he relocated from L.A. to Maine. We have some pieces by local artists who are known internationally, and some who soon will be." Karen laughed.

"At least that's my opinion. And we have regular customers from all over—some out of the country. We communicate with them through e-mail. We have our own web site now. When I say we, I mean me and Ana. You know her. We're in this together. We share in the way the art is displayed on the walls and partitions. We have a couple of artists who work through distributors. They like to come in and personally set up their artists' paintings themselves, but in general, Ana and I do it

ourselves. Aunt Pam, I'm glad I decided to open the gallery. It
was tough at first, but it's been worth it. I'm happy."

"And I'm happy for you. I know your mom is proud of you."

"Really . . ? Humph! You think so? I doubt it. I can't
remember her ever being proud of anything I've done. If she was,
she never showed it." Karen shook her head, Pam nodded hers.

"Of course she's proud of you. She talks about you all the
time. For whatever reason, I don't know, but I think, at times, it's
difficult for Frannie to show her feelings."

"Maybe to me, but she doesn't have any problem showing
her feelings to Danny. She seems to do a pretty good job of
showering him with her attention and affection. With her, he can
do NO wrong." Pamela reached over and grabbed Karen's right
hand, cupped it between her own and stroked it.

"You have to understand: he's the only boy . . . and he's the
baby. Who doesn't love the baby? Everyone does." Pamela
smiled, nodded, and waited for Karen to nod in agreement. Karen
removed her hand from Pamela's grip. She stared off into space.
She shifted her weight from side to side on the sofa and slid her
hands under her thighs.

"Not everyone," Karen replied. She turned to face Pamela
and raised an eyebrow. Pamela studied Karen's face for a while.
There was nothing to indicate that Karen was joking; there wasn't
a hint of a smile in her eyes or her mouth. And while she couldn't
tell that Karen was gritting her teeth, her pulsating jaws were clear
evidence that she was angry. Pamela sighed and nodded.

"I guess you're right. Especially if that person thinks their
share of attention is being given to that baby. Am I right?" Karen
didn't answer. "Karen, your mom is the eldest child. Do you know
what kind of pressure, along with responsibilities, that can put on
a child? A lot of times, they're expected to help out with the
younger children and set an example for them. Personally, I think
it robs them of some of their childhood. Because, after all, they are
just children themselves. Our parents were very young when they
got married and had us; Frances was like a second mother to me
and Grace. After school, she heated up or cooked our dinner and
helped us with our homework. I know it had to be rough on her to
have to have us tagging along with her everywhere, but she never

made us feel bad about it. Really, she seemed to enjoy it . . . being a big sister, having us look up to her. I think she changed after Grace was killed in that car accident. You were just a toddler then. Frannie then started acting like she wanted to fix all the woes of the world. She became very serious for a while, analyzing everything. She's gotten a lot better since then, but she's always been sort of reserved."

"Except with Danny," Karen interjected.

"We didn't have a brother, and like I said, he is the baby."

"And he always will be, so that's not very consoling."

"But she loves you too. She loves all of you."

"She has a poor way of showing it."

"She probably could have been more open, but she didn't know how. She did the best she could."

Pam looked deep into Karen's eyes. "Have you told her how you feel?" she asked.

Karen put her head down and thought about it for a long time. Telling her mother how she felt meant having a serious conversation with her; it meant opening up and putting her feelings on the line, exposing herself to possible further hurt, and Karen barely spoke to her mother.

"No," she answered.

"Then how could she possibly know where she went wrong and try to make it better? Instead, you've pulled away from her."

Karen's head flew up; she stared at Pam, wondering how she knew that she had withdrawn from her mother. She hadn't told Pam, but Pam spoke as though she were sure of her statement.

"How did you know?"

"She told me, about a year ago, that you stopped calling her and wouldn't answer her phone calls. I called you a few times to talk to you about it. I couldn't catch you so I left you messages, but you didn't return my calls either. Eventually, I gave up; I shouldn't have. Now, I feel that I'm partly responsible for your remaining distanced from your mom." Karen took a deep breath and stared into space again.

"I remember. I just got tired of everybody. I think I cut off just about everyone. I didn't return anyone's phone calls." Karen looked into Pam's face. "I remember the talks you and I had when

I was a little girl. You were always there for me; you never let me down." Karen put her head down again. "I'm sorry, Aunt Pam," Karen said, her voice just above a whisper, and breaking up. "I'm sorry I never called you back; I should have."

"There's no need to be sorry. That was in the past. We're going to start afresh. We're starting right now, and we're going to promise each other to keep in touch. Okay?"

Pamela reached out for Karen's hands again. Karen pulled her hands out from under her thighs and extended them to Pamela. They were warm. Pamela took hold of them and held them tight. Karen smiled and nodded.

Chapter Five

Danny and Lauren were in bed when Lauren did it: she brought up what was not just *a* forbidden topic, but *the* forbidden topic. They had never discussed which topics were taboo and not open to discussion, but this one, though unspoken, was understood: Karen. She didn't attend family events, and the family tried to be diplomatic when referring to Karen by not saying any unkind things in front of Lauren, but Lauren could tell there was contention between Karen and the rest of the family.

Danny had turned off the nightlight on his side of the bed and pulled in close to Lauren. He had on only his boxers; she was wearing a short silky camisole and bikini set. She was lying down on her side, facing him—and ready. That's what Danny loved about Lauren—no games. He started with a gentle kiss on her lips and a light stroke on her inner thighs. She rolled over on her back, and he got on top of her. Danny passionately kissed her mouth, chin and neck. He nudged the bottom edge of her camisole up to just above her nipples, and he slid his tongue across one of them. She giggled.

He was just about to consume her small breasts when she committed the grave error and ruined the moment. Lauren said something, and instead of inaudible sounds—which he would have loved—she said actual words. Words that didn't tie in with the moment, and were quite clear:

"Danny . . .?" she began.

"Hmm hmm," he replied.

"What is it with Karen and your family?" she asked between short breaths. Danny paused for a moment, in disbelief. He couldn't believe that she would ask such a question at that moment. It certainly wasn't a turn-on. He stared deep into her eyes but said nothing. He dismissed her question and continued his journey. He opened his mouth, surrounded the area he wanted to devour, which was nearly her entire breast, and proceeded to suck ravenously. It took every gram of strength Lauren had to prevent herself from crumbling, but she wasn't one to back down; she took risks.

"She's never at your family's functions; I only saw her once—when we first got together. I just wondered if I had anything to do with it, if I was part of the problem." Danny released his prey, raised his head and gave Lauren a blank stare.

"You? Why would you think that?"

"Because . . . I'm Black?"

"Aw, come on, Lauren," he groaned. "Are you serious? None of my family is like that—not even Karen. Now, can we go on?" Lauren gave him a sheepish grin. She didn't really think it was because of her race—or hoped it wasn't, but she did want to know what was going on with the family and their relationship with Karen. She thought she'd bring up one possible reason why Karen might be distant with the family.

"Then what is it? I want to know? I want to know about your family." She smoothed his hair down around and behind his ears. "I love you. And they are a part of you. They made you who you are. That's important to me."

"I don't want to discuss it, Lauren, and anyway, now is not the time. It seems to me that we're kind of busy here." Danny proceeded to kiss her again. He started again with her mouth and was just about to kiss her chin.

"If not now, when?" Lauren asked. Danny stopped short and sighed. He raised his head and gave her a quick look. He didn't say a word. He kissed her forehead, got off her, and laid down on his side, facing away from her. Lauren knew she had lost the battle—for now, so she didn't pursue any further discussion. Instead, she snuggled up close behind him, put her arm across his waist and whispered, "I love you." Danny nodded, indicating he knew, but said nothing. That night, and any possible activity came to an end.

Conversation between Danny and Lauren was strained for a couple of days. It consisted of what they were having for dinner and how their day went at work. During their relationship, they never went without speaking to each other; they talked things out. They weren't unkind to each other, and rarely became distant. And the one or two times they did become a little distant, it wasn't for long.

On the third day, Danny finally gave in. Lauren was his soul mate; he was sure of that. He didn't like friction between the two of them. And while most people let him have his way, he learned from Lauren that at times he too had to give in. This was one of those times. And besides that, he was horny and wanted to finish his interrupted journey.

"Good night, Danny," Lauren said as she walked past the living room where Danny was busy watching TV. Danny immediately turned the TV off and began to follow her.

"I guess I'll go to bed too," he said. Lauren went in the bathroom to brush her teeth; Danny went in and brushed his too. Lauren headed toward the bedroom, Danny followed. They entered the bedroom. Lauren took her lingerie out of the dresser and started to change. Danny watched her as she slipped into her lingerie. He scratched his head.

"About that question you asked," he began. "I'm ready to talk about it now." Lauren didn't pretend she didn't remember or know what he was talking about. She sat on the edge of the bed and motioned for him to sit next to her.

"Okay," she said. "So . . . what is going on between your family and Karen?" Danny sighed the sigh of a man with a tanker full of troubles on his shoulders. He shook his head.

"I'm not sure." He hung his head and stared at the floor. "Karen started acting different, I think, when we were teenagers. She acted like she wasn't part of the family."

"Did she have any friends?"

Danny stared in Lauren's direction but not at her. "Yes, she had friends. They came over the house, and she would go to theirs."

"Did she hang out with your sisters?"

"No, I think they thought she was too young, and Helen and

Brigit were really close."

"How about you?"

"Me? What about me?"

"Did she hang with you? Go places with you?

"No. Who wants to hang out with their sister? I hung out with the guys. I didn't even think about her."

"So . . . what you're telling me is that Karen had no one. She was all alone in a family with four kids." Those words leveled Danny like a wrecking ball striking a dilapidated building. He thought for a long time. He nodded, raised his head and looked into Lauren's eyes. He thought again, then sighed. He had never tried to figure out why Karen acted as she did in the past.

"She was close to dad," he said. "She was his favorite. And when he died . . ."

"When he died, what?" Lauren asked. Danny shook his head.

"I think that's when Karen really changed. She became distant—like a stranger. You know, we had to practically force her to visit mom when she was in the hospital." Danny put his head down again and went into deep thought.

"Danny . . . I'm sorry. Maybe I shouldn't have insisted, but I wanted to know. I needed to know. It's just that Lisa and I have always been close. Maybe because there's only the two of us. I don't know. And my family is close—we always have been. So I . . . I needed to know . . ." Danny put his head next to hers.

"It's alright. I guess I needed to know too." When Danny was hurting, he looked like a little boy to Lauren. She held his face in her hands, kissed him, and held him tight. No words were spoken.

The next morning, Danny and Lauren were back to their old selves. Danny was about to leave for work. He and Lauren were in the hallway leading to the door. Lauren had on her robe; Danny was almost finished dressing. He just needed to fix his tie. As he knotted his tie, Lauren pleaded:

"No . . . please don't leave me. Don't leave me here all alone." Danny stopped fixing his tie. He tilted his head, raised his eyebrows and smiled.

"Why, do you have something in mind?" he chuckled. Lauren laughed.

"Not really, but I still don't want you to go. She put the back

of her hand on her forehead to give a dramatic effect. "Please
don't leave me all alone," she said. Her love of old romance
movies was kicking in, and Danny fell in line.

Looking at the ceiling and then at her, Danny said, "Don't
worry, little lady, I'll be back." He then emphasized his words by
jabbing the air with his fingers and repeated, "I will be back." The
two burst into uncontrollable laughter.

"Okay . . . okay . . . enough of that," Lauren said, motioning
for him to stop, as she continued laughing. "Let's be serious for a
minute. What do you want for dinner?" Danny shrugged.

"It doesn't matter. Surprise me." He looked at his watch. It
was later than he thought. Lauren should have been dressed for
work, and she wasn't. "Are you going in this morning?" he asked.

"Yes, I'm running a little late. It'll be okay. (long pause)
Danny . . . ?

"Yes?"

"I want to see if I can get close to Karen. I would like us to be
friends."

"Why?" Danny asked. He didn't ask out of spite. It wasn't
that he disliked Karen; he had no emotional ties to her. He knew it
wasn't going to be easy for Lauren to win Karen over as a friend.
Karen did everything possible to distance herself from the family,
and Danny was sure that Karen would do the same to Lauren. He
didn't think Lauren would be up to the challenge she'd surely
face.

"I just do," Lauren answered. "And besides, I think she needs
a friend, and that she'd be a good one to have. But I wanted to find
out first if you're okay with that. I won't try without your
permission." Danny thought for a long time.

"Sure," he said. "And good luck."

"Thanks," she said as she centered his tie. "Well, then . . .
perfect! Let me hurry up and get ready." She kissed Danny and
rushed out of the hallway.

"Good luck," he called out. And then, under his breath said,
"You're gonna need it."

Chapter Six

"My feet are killing me," Pam moaned. "I'm too old for this."

"We've only been in two buildings. We have a couple more—and the gardens," Karen said, laughing. "My feet hurt too—and I'm hungry. You don't hear me complaining." The ladies had been at the Getty Center all morning, and it had taken its toll; they were dragging. Karen may not have complained, but she was worn out.

"We have two options," Pam said. "We can go home and eat, which involves walking all the way to the tram, waiting for it, taking it down the hill, taking the stairs or elevator to where the car is and then drive *all* the way home, or we can stay and eat at one of their cafes. I propose we eat here; it'll be faster." Karen agreed. Getting to the car wasn't as bad as Pam made it seem, but then they would have had to take the drive to Pam's house. Of course eating where they were would be much faster.

The small stand in the center courtyard had a long line and the seating area was nearly full. They decided to eat at the Garden Terrace Café on the lower level, because they could see from where they were, up above, that more seating was available there. The only drawback in going there was that they had to walk down four sets of steps to get to it. The steps weren't steep—only about two or three inches high–but there were about fifty-five of them. (Pam counted them out loud as they descended, and complained.) Karen reminded her that it was not a climb; they had gone *down* the stairs.

Once there, they bought a couple of sandwiches and found

outside seating near one of the square-shaped columns. They were finally able to get off their feet.

"You haven't said anything about your mom," Pam said while they were eating.

"What is there to say?"

"How is it going between you two? I know you're still going over to Helen's. Do you think your relationship is improving? Have you gotten any closer?"

Karen shrugged her shoulders.

"Not really," she admitted. "I take a movie for us to watch while I'm there. We watch the movie. We don't really talk much; we don't have anything to talk about." Pam scrunched her nose up and shook her head.

"That's not true, Karen. You two have a lot in common." She then leaned toward Karen and pointed at her." You just don't know it yet." Karen shrugged her shoulders.

"Like what, for instance? Tell me one thing," she demanded. Karen crossed her arms and leaned back, challenging Pam. If Pam was going to make a statement like that, Karen wanted Pam to come up with proof to back up her claim. Pam gave Karen a sly grin, leaned back, and shook her head.

"Oh, no, I'm not going to tell you. That's for you to find out on your own. And the only way you can do that is by talking to her. I guaranty you'll be pleasantly surprised." Pam reached over and touched Karen's hand. "Are you going to at least try?" Unwilling to commit, Karen looked away. Pam tapped Karen's hand.

"Oh, and I forgot to mention that they're planning to give your mom a birthday party next month," Pam said. "You will be there, won't you?"

"I haven't heard anything about it, so I guess I'm not invited." Karen faced Pam and looked her in the eye. "And . . . I guess that means I won't have to go." Karen gave a big smile showing all of her teeth, flitted her eyes and rocked her head from side to side. She liked the idea of not having to come up with an excuse. If she wasn't invited, she could always claim ignorance. They had stopped inviting her anyway, so it wouldn't be anything new.

"They're going to invite you. They've just started planning it; that's why I'm mentioning it now. And you can't say you didn't hear about it, because I just told you . . . Karen, you should be there."

Karen took a deep breath and looked at the stone column next to Pam. She noticed a gap in the column that indicated to her that it wasn't solid, but had been pieced together. She looked past Pam, eyed several nearby large potted plants, then the courtyard, people walking, and the beautiful scenery surrounding them, not focusing on anything in particular.

"Karen, you have to go to your mother's birthday party. There's no excuse for your not attending. None. Who knows how many more she'll have? We hope many, but who knows?"

Karen studied Pam's face, her eyes saddened by Karen's disinterest in her mother. She was moved by what she saw. She felt as though she were letting Pam down and disappointing her. "Okay . . . okay," Karen said, grimacing in pain as if someone were literally twisting her arm. "If I'm invited, I'll go." She really hoped they wouldn't invite her.

"Oh, you'll be invited," Pam assured her. Pam nodded and smiled. "Now let's finish our lunch and go home. I'm done for the day," she said. "We can go to the other buildings another time." Karen agreed.

Chapter Seven

"Mom, we're almost through with the arrangements for your birthday party. Are there any of your friends you'd like to invite?" Helen asked Frances. When she said arrangements, Helen meant that they had bought decorations, ordered a birthday cake and decided on a menu.

"Not this time, dear. Let's have just family. And don't forget to tell Karen when she comes. She should be here soon."

"Why, mom?" Helen asked with desperation in her voice.

"Why, what? Invite your sister to her mother's birthday party?" Frances asked as if she were clueless as to how Helen and Karen felt about each other. Part of the reason was that she was in denial: she couldn't accept that her own children could barely stand each other. She and her sisters were very close; she had expected, or had hoped for, the same with her children. She wanted Helen to realize how unreasonable it would be for a child not to be invited to their own mother's birthday party, but Helen couldn't see it.

"Yes, why invite someone who ruins it for everyone else by acting as if she's miserable when she's around us?"

Helen had a valid argument: Karen made it clear by the usual scowl on her face, her slouched body and lack of conversation at family gatherings that she did not want to be there. Helen felt they were better off when Karen didn't show up to dampen their spirits. But Frances refused to back down. She had hopes that one day Karen would change, and that wouldn't happen unless she were invited.

"Karen, it's my birthday party, and I would like the entire

family to be there. If Karen doesn't come, let that be her decision, but please don't eliminate her . . . Please." Helen let out a heavy sigh.

"It's up to you, mom. Like you said, 'It's your party.'"

"Thank you," Frances said, relieved that the discussion wasn't going to escalate into an argument.

"And what about now, mom? I wish you'd come with us to the movies. All you're going to do here with Karen is watch a movie. At least with us you'll get a chance to get out of the house," Helen pleaded. Brad had entered the room and overheard Helen invite Frances to go to the movies with them.

"Yeah . . . you should join us," Brad added. "You need to get out of the house sometime." Brad hadn't heard the conversation leading up to the invitation, so he didn't realize it had anything to do with Karen, and what he was stepping into.

"Thanks, Brad . . . but, no. And you may think we're just watching movies, Helen, but we're doing more than that: Karen and I are spending time together. Time is so precious, dear, and I want to give some of mine to Karen."

"Time watching a movie," Helen snapped. "That's not quality time, mom. You should be spending your time with people who love you and *want* to be with you." Recognizing the signs of a possible family argument, Brad took his cue and ran with it—as fast as possible. He exaggerated his noticing the time by holding his arm out, bending it so he could see the face of his watch, and then pointed at it. He shook his head.

"I'd better check on the boys and make sure they're ready," he said as he rushed out of the room. Brad was very serious about avoiding Andersen family issues. He limited his decision making to his little family, the Mitchell family. Since Helen was usually the decision maker with her siblings and at her job, as an exec, she was relieved and happy to have someone else take on that responsibility at home; she welcomed it.

And when Helen made decisions without consulting Brad that involved him and the boys when she and her siblings got together, Brad did not feel that his authority was being threatened. Helen's decisions were always in line with what he would've agreed to if they had discussed it in advance. The two worked together as a team, and their boys knew better than to try to play one against the other. They had tried in the past, and it didn't work. Helen and Brad maintained a united front.

"Don't worry about me, Helen," Frances said. "And who's to say Karen doesn't love me? She's never said that. Maybe she does but doesn't know how to show it. I think she does in her own way. She doesn't have to come here, but she does. No one's forcing her. No one can make her come here." Helen shook her head and sighed. She gave her mom a look and threw her hands in the air.

"I give up! I can see I'm not getting anywhere with you," Helen said. "Brigit wants you to have dinner with them tonight. She said she'll have Michael pick you up at five. Is that okay with you?"

"That will be fine, dear. In the meantime, I can spend some time with Karen." Helen and Frances stared at each other. Helen took a deep breath. She restrained herself from hurling additional words of reproof, while Frances braced herself, ready for the next negative comment. Neither said a word. The doorbell rang. The staring contest ended. Helen exhaled.

"Let me get that. It's probably her," Helen said. She went to the door and opened it. It was Karen with a DVD in hand. Helen forced a smile.

"Hello, Karen . . . it's good to see you," Helen said without a hint of enthusiasm or sincerity. They walked into the living room. Helen focused on the DVD and gave Frances a look and half nod. "I see you brought a movie to watch. How nice," Helen said as she raised an eyebrow and gave Frances another look.

"Oh, and before I forget, and while Helen's still here, dear," Frances cut in, "they're planning a birthday party for me. You will come . . . won't you?" she asked Karen.

"I guess, if I'm invited." Karen looked over at Helen to see her reaction to the invitation; she caught the end of a frown replaced with a blank expression.

"Don't be silly, Karen. Of course you're invited," Helen said, locking eyes with Frances. She then gave Frances a forced half smile.

"Then I guess it's settled: you'll be there," Frances said as she clapped her hands and lifted her head high as if she had won a major battle. Helen scanned the room; she wanted to get away fast. She looked for an imaginary exit or way of escape.

"What's taking them so long?" Helen asked herself out loud. "Brad . . . boys? I'm waiting. Come on . . . Hurry!" she called out. Brad and the boys entered the room. The boys greeted Karen and said good-bye to Frances.

"We'll be back in a few hours," Helen said. "And I hope you two enjoy the movie," she said as they exited the door. Her tone was filled with sarcasm, but Frances didn't allow it to dampen her enthusiasm over Karen's visit, and Karen simply ignored Helen's tone.

"We will," Frances called out. Frances looked over at Karen and gave her a big smile. "Well, I guess it's just us, now, Karen," she said beaming with joy. Karen headed toward the DVD player with the DVD in hand. "Before we watch the movie, I thought maybe we could talk for just a few minutes. We don't do much of that," Frances said. Karen turned to face her mother. "Tell me, dear, how was your day?" Frances asked. Karen shrugged her shoulders.

"Okay, I guess."

"What did you do?"

"Um, not much. Well . . . not anything that I think you'd find interesting, mother."

"At least give me a chance; you never know," Frances said. She stared at Karen's mouth and waited for her to say something . . . anything. Frances gave Karen a slight nod of encouragement. Karen took a deep breath.

"Okay," Karen said slightly annoyed. Karen went back to the sofa, plunked down next to Frances and placed the DVD on the table.

"Well . . . first thing this morning, I went to the gallery."

"The gallery. Yes . . . how is it coming along?"

"Coming along? Good. Ana usually opens it and I go in a little later . . . usually in the afternoon, but she had an appointment this morning, so I went in early."

"Oh, yes . . . Ana. So, you still keep in touch with her."

"She's my best friend, mother!"

"How is she doing? I haven't seen her in a long time."

"She's fine, mother." Karen cleared her throat. "She asks about you all the time."

"You should bring her by sometime. I've always liked her. She's such a sweet person."

"I know. She's always been there for me; I can always count on her."

"You've been friends for a long time." Karen agreed with a nod.

"Yes, since grade school. But enough of her, mother. You asked about the gallery: it's going great. We're adding works from a new artist, and we're planning a special exhibition of some of her pieces. I'm really excited about it."

"Maybe I can go."

"You?" Karen said in disbelief. She leaned back and stared at Frances, wondering why she would be interested in going to see some art.

"Yes, Karen . . . I appreciate art. I *love* art." Karen crossed her arms and threw her head back.

"Oh, really? Since when?"

"Since before you were born, dear," Frances said with a great deal of indignation. Sociology was my major in college, but I minored in Art."

"You minored in Art? I didn't know that. Why . . . why didn't you tell me?" Karen asked with controlled excitement and disbelief. She leaned in to hear the explanation. This was news to her, and she wanted to know why this important piece of information was withheld from her. Frances shrugged her shoulders.

"I don't know. I just didn't. When I first discovered that you were interested in art, I was ecstatic. I didn't want you to feel any pressure to pursue your interest in art because of me, so I kept quiet and waited. I waited to see if it was just a passing fancy, and when you were a senior in high school and told your dad and me that you wanted to pursue a career in art, I was overjoyed."

"But you never said anything. You didn't say a word." Karen wrinkled her forehead and blinked as if to remove debris from her eyes.

"That isn't exactly true; I always tried to be very supportive.

And I never said anything negative about your decision. Think about it." Frances paused for a moment to give Karen a chance to think back.

Karen thought for a long minute. While her mother hadn't said anything negative about her decision to pursue art, she hadn't encouraged her to pursue it either. She wondered if that's what she meant by being supportive.

"I am so proud of you. I used to be in the art world myself. I've been to all of the local museums and art galleries. Well . . . so have you. I took you children when you were very young. Surely you haven't forgotten that. And when we went on family vacations, we always included going to at least one art museum or gallery. You don't know it, but I used to paint a little myself."

"But I don't understand why you didn't say anything," Karen said with heightened interest and excitement.

"I didn't want to influence you at all; I wanted your decision to pursue art to be completely your own." Frances folded her arms and lifted her head with a sense of extreme pride. "I'll have you know that you inherited your love of art from me."

"And that's all," Karen said. "Just your love of it, because I'm not artistic at all."

"Maybe you didn't give yourself enough time to fully develop it. I always loved your art; it was unique. You know there are some people who aren't traditional artists—there always have been. That could be the case with you. And most artists who are considered to be great now weren't appreciated during their own lifetime. I know you learned that in art history. Think about it." Karen shrugged.

"I don't know," Karen said in a tone detecting that she was unconvinced that she might have any artistic ability that might be appreciated by anyone other than a mother. Karen sighed.

"Don't give up: it's not too late. Now, tell me about the type of art you carry in the gallery." Her mother's background and love of art was a lot for Karen to take in. She looked at Frances as though she were seeing her through a magnifying glass: every detail clearly visible. There was so much to take in—and to talk about. She was dumbfounded.

"Okay," Karen said, "but you're going to have to come in

and see for yourself." That was the beginning of a lengthy and engaging conversation between mother and daughter. Time went by fast as they talked about a mutual love: art. They were still engrossed in conversation when Helen and the family returned.

"How was the movie," Helen asked Frances while ignoring Karen's very presence.

"Movie?" Frances glanced at the TV that had not been turned on and the DVD on the table. "Oh, we didn't get a chance to watch the movie." Frances touched Karen's arm. "I'm sorry, Karen. Maybe we can watch it next time."

"No, mother, it's okay," Karen said. Karen reached for and grabbed the DVD. "It's a rental. I have to return it before next week."

"I'm truly sorry, dear."

"It's okay, mother," Karen repeated. "Don't worry about it. It's nothing."

Helen stood still and looked back and forth at the two with her mouth opened. She had no choice but to acknowledge Karen's existence. She stared at Karen and waited for an explanation as to why they didn't watch the DVD, and what they did instead. Karen ignored her.

"I'd better go," Karen said. "Ana's waiting for me so she can leave for her appointment. I'll tell her you asked about her. I'll see you later." Karen got up and headed towards the door.

"I had a good time," Frances called out.

"I did too, mother," Karen said over her shoulder. Helen closed her mouth and continued to stare. She followed Karen to the door.

"Oh, and I'll see you later, Helen," Karen said as she glanced in Helen's direction. Helen nodded and gently closed the door behind Karen. She raced back to the living room with Frances.

"What was that about?" Helen whispered to Frances.

"What was what about?"

"You said you had a good time and you didn't watch the movie? What did you do?" Helen took a quick look around the room for evidence of their having played cards or board games. There was none. She was stumped.

"Oh . . . Karen and I, we talked," Frances said.

"You talked?" Helen asked in disbelief.

"Yes, we just talked." Frances nodded and gave a smile of a woman with a secret.

Helen wondered how her mother could get Karen to open up and have a conversation with her when Karen barely said more than "hi" and "bye" to the rest of the family. And her mother's conversation with Karen had to have lasted for hours, because Helen and the family had been gone that long. Helen considered a lengthy conversation with Karen to be a next-to-impossible feat. She had to know more.

"What did you talk about?"

"Oh . . . we talked about things: things we have in common." Frances didn't offer any further information, and Helen could tell by the smug look on Frances' face and the way she said it, matter-of-factly, and with finality as though she were through that Frances had said all she was going to say on that subject. She wasn't going to get any more information from her. Helen decided not to pursue it and ask for more. With a blank expression having settled on her face, Helen shrugged her shoulders and nodded.

Chapter Eight

Karen went directly to the gallery. There were a few people milling around. For a small gallery, it did well. Being located close to several larger and popular galleries no doubt helped business; that gave her walk-in business, but Karen also had gained clients by word of mouth. Because of her keen eye as to what would sell, she had a lot of return business. And she regularly rotated paintings displayed with some kept in storage so that the gallery's presentation never got stale.

Karen had some interior decorators that regularly stopped by the gallery to see what she had. They regularly sought artwork at her gallery; she had made it on their list of galleries to regularly check. And she appreciated it.

"How's it going," Karen asked Ana.

"Pretty good so far. Raquel came in this morning and bought a couple of paintings for a house she's decorating. And that one's getting a lot of attention. I've had several people ask about it." Ana pointed at a large painting of a pair of horses—one black and one white—grazing on a luxuriant field near an enclosure filled with horses eating on bales of hay. Karen folded her arms as though she were hugging herself, closed her eyes and took a deep breath. This was a popular piece: a lot of people gazed at and studied it, but no one had purchased it.

"I feel good about adding her art to the gallery. And she approached ME, asking if she could display some here. I'm glad she did. I know the exhibition is going to be a success. I've already had some people confirm that they are coming, so I know we'll have a few people . . . Oh . . . and mother told me to tell you

she asked about you and that she hopes you'll stop by to see her."
Ana gave Karen a puzzled look and shook her head.

"What . . ?

"Didn't you tell her I asked about her?" Ana questioned.

"Yes."

"It's not my fault I haven't been by to see your mom. You hadn't been by to see her yourself for a long time, Karen. So how could I possibly see her? Was I supposed to go without you?" Ana had tried on many occasions to persuade Karen to visit or call her mother, but she refused. Her insistence had reached the point to where their friendship seemed to be in jeopardy, so Ana eased up and from time to time would only ask how Karen's mother was doing. She no longer suggested that Karen call or visit.

"I'm just relating the message, Ana." Karen patted Ana's shoulder. "Calm down. Don't you have an appointment to go to?" Ana looked at the clock on the wall; she sucked her teeth.

"Yeah . . . and if I'm gonna make it, I guess I'd better leave now. We'll talk about this later." She rolled her eyes at Karen, turned to leave, stopped, and then turned around. "Oh, by the way . . . Jerry stopped by."

"What did he want?" Karen asked, her voice lacking any interest.

"What do you think?" Ana retorted. Karen shrugged her shoulders. Ana rolled her eyes again and shook her head.

"Karen, you know what he wanted. He wanted to see you. Why are you torturing the man like this? Just go out with him. He's fine, rich, and . . . and he loves art. What more could you want?"

"If I were looking for someone . . . nothing. But I'm not. I'm busy, Ana. I don't have time for Jerry or any other man. I don't know why I can't get that through to you."

"Well, when you finally decide you have the time and he's taken, don't come crying to me."

"Believe me, I won't," Karen snapped back.

"Okay, then don't." It was a standoff; the girls stared at each other and refused to blink. Ana rolled her eyes. She took a quick look at the clock again.

"You know what? I've gotta go. I don't want to waste any

more time on this subject." She turned to leave.

"Ana . . ?" Karen began, her tone changing from a corrosive-type of bitter to sugary sweet. Ana stopped, turned around again, and waited for Karen to finish what she was saying. "Let's get together tonight. Do you want to go out for dinner?"

"No, not tonight, Ana answered with a hint of disgust." That's not what Karen wanted to hear. She wanted to talk to Ana, and she wanted to do it that day. But their conversation had left Ana frustrated. Going out to dinner with Karen was not inviting.

"Then, you can just come over, and we can eat in. I can order a pizza and we can watch a movie. I rented one to watch with mother, but we ended up talking the entire time. I want to tell you about my visit, and if you want . . . we can talk about Jerry too. Okay?" Karen brought up Jerry as a bargaining tool. Ana had been trying to get Jerry and Karen together for a while and Karen refused to cooperate. Karen would always change the subject whenever Ana brought up Jerry's name, so Karen thought Ana might jump at the chance of at least talking about Jerry with her.

"What makes you think I don't have plans tonight with Javi? You want me to break my plans with *my* boyfriend to talk to you about a guy that you're not even interested in?" Ana pointed at herself when she said, "*my* boyfriend," and then folded her arms and wagged her head. Karen knew Ana was right, but there was no harm in trying. She had to accept that Ana had a life of her own and could possibly have other plans. Karen shrugged her shoulders and accepted defeat.

"I didn't know you had plans with Javier. I'm sorry."

"I don't, but it's just the point that I could've." Ana rolled her eyes and frowned. Karen laughed. She grabbed Ana and hugged her. That's why you're my best friend."

"Why? Because I don't have plans with Javi?"

"No . . . because even if you did, I know you'd break it for me—if it was important." Ana didn't deny it. She tried to think of something witty to say, but couldn't.

"Well, anyway, I think Javi has a game he's gonna watch with his friends tonight. There's always some kind of game on."

"Good. Then it works out for me. Come by and let's talk." Ana nodded. She gave Karen a little shove.

"Now let me go or I'll be late for sure." Ana dashed out of the gallery.

* * *

"Don't start the movie yet," Ana pleaded. "Let's talk first." Karen and Ana were in the living room sitting on the sofa. They were all set up to watch the movie: they each had a slice of pizza on a paper plate and a glass of fruit punch. The movie was in the DVD player, waiting for the "play" button to be pushed. Karen bit into a slice of pizza, caught the trailing cheese with her fingers and popped it into her mouth.

"Okay . . . about what?" Karen asked as she chomped on the pizza.

"About Jerry."

"What about him?"

"Karen, the man has been trying to go out with you for a long time. Are you going to go out with him . . . or what?" Karen took a couple of more bites of pizza and pointed at her mouth, full of pizza. Karen had agreed to talk about Jerry, but to her, talking about him was not a priority; he was not what she wanted to talk about. Her mother was. But for that to happen, Karen knew she was going to have to let Ana have her way by first discussing Jerry. It was a tradeoff. That's why they were best friends: they knew the rules and followed them. She chewed slowly, rocked her head from side to side as though it was the best pizza she'd ever tasted, and swallowed.

"You didn't answer me. Are you going to go out with Jerry?"

"I don't know," Karen replied.

"You already went out with him a couple of times. Didn't you have a good time?" Ana asked. Karen thought for a minute. Jerry had taken her out to dinner and to the movies, and yes, they did have a good time together. Ana knew that, because Karen had told her. Asking the question was just Ana's way of reminding Karen of that fact.

"Yes, I enjoyed being with him."

Ana threw her hands up in the air, nearly losing her grip on her slice of pizza.

"Then what's the problem?" she asked. Karen squinted her eyes as she tried to figure out what the problem truly was.

"I think Jerry wants more from the relationship than I'm willing to give right now," Karen answered. "I think he wants a serious one, and . . . I don't. I'm not ready."

"And why aren't you ready?" Karen shrugged her shoulders.

"I don't know, and I don't feel like trying to figure it out. And I don't have the time right now anyway. The gallery is taking up a lot of my time; that's my number one priority. And now I'm spending some of my time visiting mother." Her mother. There! That was the topic Karen wanted to talk about, and she thought that was the tie-in to do it. Not so, because Ana wasn't ready yet. She hadn't finished trying to convince Karen to go out with Jerry, and she wasn't going to allow Karen to go onto another subject until she did.

"You could go out with him a few more times, and if you see that he's getting too serious, you could back off," Ana said. "It's just a date. It's not like I'm asking you to marry the guy."

"I know, but he's so, um . . . attentive. That's the only way I can describe it. I feel like I'm being smothered. You know: opening the car door, well . . . every door, and pulling my chair out—and then in. You know . . . so mannerly."

"And you've got a problem with that, girlfriend? It's called 'being a gentleman.'" Ana gave a long sigh. "Karen, you need help. Most women want to be given special attention. What's up with you, girl? Just give the man a chance. Okay?" Ana pouted. It almost always worked with Karen; Ana considered it to be her secret weapon. She was good at it: the sad eyes, crinkled nose and the hanging lip.

"Please . . .?"

"Okay. Okay," Karen giggled, "but I don't understand why it's so important to you; why you're so persistent. My going out with him has nothing to do with you. You have nothing to gain."

"I want you to be happy, and I think he'll make you happy." Karen jumped on that statement right away. Clearly, to make someone happy, you have to do more than just go out with them on a date, and she had made it clear to Ana that she wasn't interested in being in a relationship.

"So you're talking about more than a date. Are you talking about a relationship?"

"No . . .no, no, maybe that came out wrong. I'm just saying you could use one more friend, and Jerry could be that friend. Okay . . ? Women have men friends too."

Karen raised an eyebrow and looked at her suspiciously. She thought for a moment. Yes, women do have men friends, she thought. She knew some who did. It seemed to work for them, and they were long-lasting friendships, strong relationships.

"Okay," Karen said. She stared at Ana.

"Okay, what?"

"Okay, I'll go out with him once." Karen raised her finger to indicate "one." Ana nodded. "Now, on to what I want to talk about." Ana nodded and waved her hand, signaling that it was okay for Karen to continue.

"When I visited my mother today, Ana, I think we connected."

"I knew it! You see? I told you if you gave your mom a chance you two could get close."

"Wait! I didn't say we got close. I said we connected, we clicked. I found out that she loves art too. We both love art! Can you believe it? According to her, I got it from her. We had an interesting conversation. And she wants to come to the gallery."

"I've been trying to tell you to get together with your mom. You have to give her a chance. Family is important, girl. With my family, we could hate each other's guts, but when we have our family get-togethers, everyone shows up. We don't distance ourselves; we're there for each other—and there are a lot of us—with all my aunts, uncles, cousins, second cousins . . ."

"Ana, don't," Karen interrupted. "My connecting with my mother has nothing to do with the others. To me, we just grew up in the same house; there are no ties."

"Maybe in time you'll change your mind. I hope so." Ana felt sorry for Karen. She couldn't imagine being without her family. To her, it would be like a kitten being separated from the rest of its litter: lost and lonely. She didn't want Karen to remain that way, but she realized there was nothing she could do. It was up to Karen to make the change.

"Don't count on it. They're giving mother a birthday party, and I'm invited. I'm sure I'm last on the list. Once again, I'll be the outsider. I promised I'd go, but I can assure you it won't be fun for me; it never is."

"Not if you think like that upfront. And people can sense negative vibes, Karen. Just give it a try, and give Jerry a try. You'll see. I'm sure." Karen gave Ana a reluctant half nod.

* * *

Karen arrived late at the party—as usual. She had hoped that by the time she got there they would be in the middle of their festivities and wouldn't notice her arrival. Then she could quickly greet her mother, so she'd know she was there, eat a slice of cake and leave. That was the plan, but they were running behind schedule.

When Karen entered the house, Frances ran over to her and hugged her as if she were the guest of honor. Karen felt embarrassed. She talked to her mother for a little while and then waved to Pam across the room. She greeted the others and found an empty chair, in a corner, to sit and hopefully, avoid having to deal with anyone. Instead of being left alone, Karen's brothers-in-law, Michael and Brad, went over to greet her and tried to engage her in small talk. As usual, she kept the conversation short.

Also at the party were Helen and her family, of course, since it was their house, Brigit and her family, Danny and Lauren, and Pamela with her husband Scott. After chatting with Brad and Michael, Karen scanned the room: everyone seemed to be busy talking. She checked to see that no one else was coming in her direction or looking her way. They weren't. She got up and darted into the kitchen, where she could be alone. Lauren had been eyeing Karen from across the room. She saw Karen's quick escape, and followed her.

"Hi," Lauren said, catching Karen off guard. Karen turned around to find Lauren at her heels. "I'm Lauren, Danny's girlfriend." Lauren extended her hand to shake Karen's. Karen gave her a limp handshake and stared at her as if she were trying to read her face.

"I've seen you before," Karen announced.

"Yes, I met you a while back at another family dinner."

"No," Karen said as she vigorously pointed her finger at Lauren and shook her head. Karen eyed Lauren up and down. "I've seen you . . . in the gallery—a number of times." Lauren put her head down and looked at Karen through the corner of her eye. She had hoped that by dropping her head, Karen wouldn't know for sure it was her, and possibly dismiss it, thinking she saw someone who looked like her. She certainly didn't want Karen to think she had been spying on her.

"Yes, I've been there a few times," Lauren confessed. Karen's eyes lit up.

"I remember that Ana, my partner, approached you one day to see what kind of art you liked, and you said you were browsing." Karen snapped her fingers. "Yes, I remember you. You spend a lot of time looking at the painting with the two horses." Lauren was caught; she couldn't deny it. She raised her head and gave Karen a half smile.

"I didn't realize I was so obvious," Lauren said. "Then I guess I should just be upfront with you. I go to the gallery because I enjoy looking at your art—especially that painting, and the reason I followed you in here is because I thought we might get a chance to know each other."

"Why?" Karen asked as she raised her opened hands and hunched her shoulders.

"I thought that since it seems that one day I'll be a part of this family, we could be friends." Karen moved in close to Lauren. She cupped her hand at the side of her mouth and whispered close to Lauren's ear.

"Then you've come to the wrong person, Lauren, because I'm not a part of this family. I'm as much an outsider as you are. Better yet, you're probably more a part of this family than I am." Karen then turned away and left the kitchen. She headed back toward the others. But Lauren wasn't through; she stayed on Karen's heels.

"I would still like us to be friends. Maybe we can chat the next time I'm in the gallery--if you're not busy." Karen tilted her head and shrugged her shoulders.

"Hey . . . you never know," Karen said as she re-entered the room with the others. That was all Lauren needed to hear. That answer left the door open, because Karen didn't say no. And Lauren held her to it. It wasn't too long after that unintended invitation that Karen saw Lauren hanging around the gallery like a homeless kitten seeking shelter from the rain. And it wasn't too long after that that the two women became friends. Lauren made regular visits to the gallery, and she and Karen would spend some time talking.

At times, Danny accompanied Lauren to the gallery when he and Lauren had plans immediately after her visit with Karen. Instead of staying in the car, he'd go in the gallery with Lauren. When the two women would start talking, he'd excuse himself and view art on a different wall, in another corner. In the meantime, Karen learned to tolerate Danny's presence. They did not speak to each other—no verbal communication—but they did acknowledge each other's presence with a slight tilt of their heads.

Chapter Nine

The time finally arrived for the exhibition at the gallery. Karen expected to be busy most of the day, so she asked Helen to drop Frances off for a couple of hours. That would give Frances enough time to look at the art and steal some time with Karen.

Karen did not see Frances when she entered the gallery. While talking to a customer, she caught her mother across the way smiling proudly at her. It was a look that Karen couldn't recall ever seeing in her mother before, and it was one that, for the moment, she wanted to bask in, like the warm sunlight through a window on a chilly day. She went over to greet Frances. By then, they had reached the point of embracing when seeing each other. Frances had always hugged Karen, but now, Karen was hugging Frances too.

"Mother, I'm glad you could make it," Karen said. "Let me give you a quick tour; then, you can look on your own." Karen pointed at a chair behind the counter. "We put a chair there in case you become tired."

"Where is Ana?" Frances asked as she looked around. Ana was busy chatting with a customer near a table they had set up with hors d'oeuvres, champagne and soda. A friend of Karen's and Ana's was keeping an eye on the table. Ana caught sight of Frances and immediately excused herself from the customer to rush over to Frances. Ana hugged Frances, then touched her cheeks next to Frances', puckered her lips and sounded a kiss. She then grabbed Frances' hands and stepped back to eye Frances from head to toe.

"Mrs. Andersen, it's so good to see you. You look good."

Ana released Frances' hands, nodded and put her hands on her hips. "You look really good, Mrs. Andersen," Ana said.

"Thanks, and you're looking as beautiful as ever, my dear," Frances said. Ana blushed; she grabbed Frances' hands.

"Karen told me you asked about me," Ana said. "I'm doing great. I'm happy where I'm at. Maybe we'll get to see more of each other now that you're feeling better. I'd like that."

"I hope I won't have to wait until I come to the gallery to see you again. You are always welcome to visit me," Frances said. Karen jumped in and separated the women's hands with a playful karate chop.

"You can talk about that later, mother. Let me show you around."

"I'll talk to you later, dear," Frances said to Ana as Karen carted her away.

"Okay," Ana called out as she focused on the customer she had promised to return to earlier. She headed back over to the customer and resumed her conversation with him. Later, when Frances decided to rest for a while, Ana and Frances were able to chat a little longer under Karen's watchful eye.

It was later in the afternoon, after Frances had gone and the gallery was nearly empty of visitors for the exhibition, that Karen sensed someone was behind her. She had been admiring one of the paintings when she felt his presence. She pretended not to notice so the person would move on, but he didn't. It was Jerry. She turned around to find him standing behind her, taking her in. Embarrassed by his gaze, she avoided eye contact.

"Karen . . ." he began, after determining that she was not going to look at him and acknowledge his presence, "I'm glad I caught up with you. I've been by a few times hoping I . . . we could have lunch together, but could never catch you." Karen had no choice but to give him eye contact. Her eyes locked with his for a quick second, then she looked in the general area of his face.

"Yes . . . Ana told me you came by, but I was busy preparing for the exhibition." Jerry scanned the area and nodded.

"And it looks like it was a success," he said. "Congratulations!" Jerry paused and moved in closer to her. Karen took a half-step back. To her, he was a little too close.

"Now that it's out of the way, you don't have any excuse," Jerry said. He smiled. "So . . . when are we going to have lunch?"

Karen looked over in Ana's direction. Ana was across the room with her arms crossed, head tilted, and one eyebrow raised. Karen knew what Ana was doing with her feet, but she looked anyway. Sure enough, she was tapping her right foot. Karen nodded and sighed.

"My schedule is currently open, Jerry. Whenever you say. Just give me a call." That answer was supposed to give Jerry just enough hope to go away, and then Karen thought she would figure out how to avoid him in the future. But Jerry didn't fall for that. Karen nodded again and turned to walk away.

"Great," he said. "I'll pick you up tomorrow at noon." Karen stopped in her tracks, turned around and stared at him.

"Tomorrow?" Karen tried to think of an excuse as to why she couldn't go to lunch. She didn't expect him to suggest having lunch so soon. She figured most people had their schedules planned at least a week in advance. She wondered how he was able to fit her in his schedule so soon. Had someone cancelled on him, or had he penciled her in assuming she'd be available? She wondered, but dared not ask.

"Yes, tomorrow," he repeated and smiled. "You said your schedule was open." Karen nodded. There wasn't anything else she could say; he was right.

"Yes . . . I did. I just didn't think you were going to say so soon." Silence. Jerry didn't offer an explanation. And he didn't apologize for wanting to have lunch so soon. "Okay, Jerry, I'll see you then," Karen said. Having accomplished his goal, Jerry smiled and left. Karen followed him with her eyes. When he was no longer in sight, she returned her attention to the gallery. Ana was no longer across the room; she was by her side.

"Well?" Ana asked.

"Well, what?" Karen answered with a blank expression on her face. Ana nudged Karen's shoulder.

"You know what I want, girl: The 4-1-1. When are you going out with him?"

"I told him I'd have lunch with him tomorrow." Karen frowned.

"Is that a bad thing? Karen, you're gonna have a good time with Jerry; he's such a sweet guy." Ana became dreamy-eyed. She started envisioning Karen and Jerry together as a happy couple, walking hand in hand. She was thinking how grateful they would be to her because she insisted that Karen go out with him.

"Snap out of it, Ana," Karen said as she snapped her fingers in front of Ana's face. Karen imagined what Ana was thinking. Ana was jolted out of her daydream. She laughed and moved Karen's fingers aside.

"I do get carried away sometimes, don't I?"

"Yes, you do." Karen rolled her eyes at Ana. "And I wish you'd stop it."

"But I do think he would be a good person to go out with," Ana said. She stared at Karen and waited for her to agree. Karen shrugged her shoulders.

"You're probably right." Ana gave Karen a look. Karen sighed.

"I know you're right. I told you I did enjoy the other times we went out, and I did. He's attractive, rich, and a very nice guy. I don't know . . . I just wonder why he's interested in me. I'm . . . "

"I don't want to hear you say anything negative about yourself, Karen." If no one else stood up for Karen, Ana always did. And now she had to do it against Karen herself. "You're attractive, smart, a good person, and one day you'll be rich too!" Karen frowned and shook her head.

"I'm not attractive." Karen was honest with herself—maybe too honest, because she was overly critical. She wasn't what people call beautiful, but she was attractive in its purest form. She wore very little makeup—usually just lip gloss—and usually wore her shoulder length, slightly wavy, blonde hair either in a ponytail, loose bun, or just hanging loose. She had a clean, wholesome look; a natural glow.

"Yes, you are," Ana insisted.

"Thank you, Ana . . . if you say so. And me, rich? Well . . . maybe not rich, but I will be successful. And it will be with your help."

"You're already successful, and you need to recognize that. Look . . . you have your own art gallery. Wake up, girl. Now, all you have to do is to get rich—or marry rich." Karen shook her finger in Ana's face.

"You see? I told you . . ." Karen began.

"Calm down, Karen," Ana laughed. "I'm kidding. I'm just kidding." Karen rolled her eyes at Ana and shook her head.

"It's not funny," Karen said.

"Yes it is," Ana said, and laughed again. "It is funny."

* * *

It was eleven thirty. Fifteen minutes had passed since the last time Karen had looked at the gallery clock to check the time. She had a half hour before Jerry was supposed to pick her up for lunch. She paced a little and stormed over to Ana. Ana was at the counter rustling through a small stack of invoices. She caught a glimpse of Karen heading her way so she picked up one of the invoices, brought it up close to her face and stared at it as though she were concentrating on the numbers. Karen walked up to her and put her hand in front of the invoice, blocking Ana's view. Ana looked at Karen, raised an eyebrow, and then stared at Karen's hand. Karen removed her hand.

"Ana, I was thinking about how you coerced me into going out with Jerry, and I resent it. I'm going out with him against my will. I'm letting you know now that I'm obligated to go out with him just one time." Karen raised her finger to signal "one." "And I'm telling you that I don't want to go out with him," she protested.

"I know, Karen, but you did give your word, and you always keep your word. I love that about you." Ana smiled; Karen rolled her eyes, then crossed her arms.

"Well . . . I'm just letting you know." Ana put the invoice down and hugged Karen.

"Girl, it'll be all right. I don't know why you're making such a big deal. It's just one date." Ana raised her finger to signal "one," and smiled. Ana then went back to the invoices. She put her head down and busied herself again with them to avoid further discussion and possible cancellation of the lunch by Karen. To Ana, the conversation was over. Ana knew to limit what she said.

While Karen did say she'd go out with Jerry one time, it didn't have to be then; she could always postpone it until another day. Ana knew that.

A customer walked in and started browsing. Ana was relieved. He could create a temporary diversion until Jerry arrived. Ana held up a few invoices and waved them in front of Karen's face.

"I'm kind of busy here," she whispered to Karen. "Maybe you could help the gentleman." Karen gave Ana a look and went over to assist the customer. Karen was still conversing with the customer when Jerry arrived.

There was no denying that Jerry was a very attractive man. Karen would have to be blind not to see that. But Jerry acted as though he didn't know—or care that he was handsome. Karen liked that about him though she wouldn't admit it. And although she didn't want to enter into a "relationship" with him, there were qualities Jerry possessed that she had noticed and found attractive: he didn't flaunt his wealth; he came across like an average guy. He was a genuinely nice guy. He had gorgeous green eyes that sometimes looked blue, depending on what he was wearing. His taste in clothing was impeccable—casual, but well fitting.

The only flaw Karen saw in Jerry, which she felt made him even more attractive, were a few strands of his sandy brown hair in front, on top, that refused to co-operate with the rest; they went their own way. Karen took a quick look in his direction. Those strands had rebelled again and won. Jerry was talking to Ana. He and Karen shared a quick smile. He continued talking to Ana until the customer left.

"Ready?" Jerry asked Karen as soon as the customer stepped outside the door and was no longer in earshot. Karen nodded. "What do you feel like eating?" he asked.

"I want . . . You know what? I want a salad," Karen answered. "But not a small one—I want a dinner-size salad. I've been craving one for a few days, and I'm hungry; I didn't eat breakfast."

"Perfect! I know a place that makes great salads and some darned good sandwiches. That's what I want. I'll take you there." Jerry motioned with his hand for Karen to head toward the door.

"I won't keep her too long," he said to Ana as he held the door open for Karen.

Jerry hovered over Karen at a safe distance (a half-step back) as they walked to his car. It was a short walk to his car, but during that time, Karen experienced a strange feeling. She didn't feel as though he were smothering her; she felt as though she were under his protective care. She felt safe and secure. Her father had been the only person that made her feel that way, and after his death, she took on the role as her own protector. When they got to Jerry's car, he opened the door for her as she knew he would. She got in.

The restaurant was nearby. On their way there, they talked about that day and how it had gone so far for them. When Jerry pulled the car into the valet area at the restaurant, he leaned over to her before he got out of the car, and asked her to wait until he went around and opened the door for her.

"I'm a big girl," she said. "I can open the door for myself." Karen reached for the door handle. Jerry gently tugged at her elbow. She turned to face him.

"Please wait for me to open the door. I know you're capable of doing it yourself, but I want to do that for you. Okay?" Jerry asked. Karen wanted to assert her independence, but he asked with such sincerity that she couldn't. Instead, she nodded. She felt her face become a little flushed, and hoped it wasn't visible.

The eager valet made a dash for her door after opening Jerry's door. He opened it and held his hand out to help her out of the car. Karen ignored the extended hand and stayed in the car until Jerry went around and extended his hand to help her out. She accepted it and exited the car. The valet gave Jerry a quizzical look and shrugged his shoulders. Jerry smiled.

When the restaurant hostess led them to their table, Jerry pulled Karen's chair out for her and gently nudged it in, behind the back of her legs, for her to sit down. After she looked over the menu, he asked her what she wanted to order. She wasn't surprised when Jerry ordered for the two of them. But what did surprise her was herself: she wasn't annoyed by it. She didn't cut him off and order for herself, but allowed him to do it. She appreciated the attention and special treatment. She enjoyed every minute of it.

During the meal, their mutual love of art was just one of many common interests she and Jerry were able to talk about over lunch. His parents were art investors. Some of their collections were on loan to museums throughout the United States. When he told her about some of them, she remembered having seen one collection.

When Jerry asked if he could take her out again, she said yes without hesitation. And when they returned to the gallery and he helped her out of the car and went towards her to kiss her, it was like the last spoonful of a delicious dessert: extremely satisfying. It was the perfect ending for a date. It was a quick kiss with a comforting hug. He walked her to the gallery door, opened it for her, waved to Ana and left. After he left, Karen continued to feel his embrace, although quick, and to smell his cologne for the remainder of the day.

"Info," Ana called out as soon as Karen entered the gallery and Jerry drove off. She darted over alongside Karen.

"What info do you want?" Ana crossed her arms and gave Karen a look.

"What info do you think I want? Not the weather or traffic. How was the date?" Karen was nonchalant. She tried to hide her enthusiasm. She felt a little guilty because Ana had to insist that she go out with Jerry, and then she ended up having a good time.

"It was nice. I had a nice time," she answered. That was an understatement, because she had a great time. Inside, she was about to explode with excitement.

"Nice? Girl, I saw him kiss you. And I could be wrong—which I doubt, but it seemed like you enjoyed it." Karen gave a sheepish grin and nodded. She wrapped her arms around herself, closed her eyes and smiled for a quick second. She opened her eyes.

"Ana, I'm glad I went out with him. Jerry's a really nice guy. I'm glad I listened to you." Ana patted Karen's shoulder.

"I'm glad too, but you didn't listen to me, girl. Dios mio! I practically had to force you." Karen laughed as she thought back on the hard time she had given Ana.

"I know, and I'm glad you did."

Jerry and Karen went out together regularly after that lunch.

They became very close. Their friendship grew into caring for each other and an unspoken understanding that they were a couple. In time, Jerry invited Karen to meet his parents, and she did, but she did not reciprocate by having him meet Frances. Though Jerry hinted, and eventually asked, about meeting Karen's mother, Karen wouldn't hear of it. She came up with a number of excuses as to why it was not a good time to meet her. Karen was not ready to travel that road—not yet. That was despite the fact that during that time, Karen and Frances had also become very close. Karen looked forward to her regular visits and conversations with her mother; they just never included talking about Jerry.

Chapter Ten

Karen and Lauren were sitting in a restaurant booth having lunch when Lauren figured it was the perfect time to put her plan into motion. It actually wasn't her plan; it was Danny's, but Lauren was all for it. Danny wanted Lauren to invite Karen over for dinner.

First, she had to prepare herself for possible rejection from Karen, which she did. Then, she had to muster up enough courage to do it. It took some doing, but she was ready.

When conversing, it was understood between the two ladies that, other than Frances, the entire family was off limits as topics for conversation—that included Danny. Just because Karen tolerated his presence in the same room, when in the gallery, didn't mean that she thought he was a suitable topic for discussion. Lauren knew that, and she knew she was about to step into what might end up being quicksand, because she was not only going to talk about him, but suggest that Karen be in his home, in his presence, eating with him, which more than likely would include having to talk to him.

Lauren had tread on similar dangerous ground in the past when she brought up the conversation about Karen and the family to Danny. She didn't back down then, and she wasn't about to this time either. Lauren cleared her throat.

"Karen, I want you to come over Saturday for dinner," she said. Immediately, Karen became suspicious: she figured Lauren was up to something. She had never been to Lauren's house; they had always gotten together at her house or in a public location.

"Why? What's happening?" Karen asked matter-of-factly so

Lauren wouldn't be aware of her suspicion and therefore answer truthfully. If there was a hidden agenda, Karen wanted it to be out in the open.

"Nothing . . . It's just that I always go to your house, and I thought maybe you could come over to mine this time. We can watch a movie and I'll fix dinner . . . Please?" Karen put her guard up and became even more suspicious. After all, Lauren lived with Danny, so that was at least one person she didn't want to be bothered with. She tolerated Danny's presence when he went to the gallery with Lauren—that was enough. Unless Danny was out of town on vacation—which he would never do without Lauren, or on a business trip, which his job rarely required, Danny would be there.

"Who's going to be there?" she asked cautiously. She gave a fake smile and waited for Lauren to say Danny, so she could decline, because Danny was one too many.

"Just Danny. He asked me to invite you, he wants you to come," Lauren spat out in one breath. Karen's jaw dropped. She didn't expect that answer. She was in a state of shock. Minor, but nonetheless a state of shock.

"He . . . asked you to invite me? Why?"

"He wants the two of you to settle your differences." Karen frowned and vigorously shook her head.

"I'm not up to any confrontation, Lauren, so why don't we just skip it."

"It's not like that at all. He feels that he is responsible for the distance between you two, and he wants to change it; he wants to make it better. All he's asking is that you two can be like brother and sister again."

Still in disbelief, Karen took a couple of seconds to digest what Lauren said. "He feels responsible? Then why hasn't he called me so we could discuss it?"

"Karen, he's afraid you won't take his call, and I know you well enough now to know that you wouldn't. Please, Karen . . . please come over for dinner." Karen began looking around, searching for something to focus on. She wasn't about to commit to going to Danny's house and eat with him. She refused to do that.

To Karen's surprise, Lauren hopped out from her side of the booth, sprinted over to Karen's side, and slid in next to her. She put her head next to Karen's and hugged her neck.

"Please?" she begged and then waited for an answer. Karen glanced at nearby tables to see if anyone was looking. They were.

"People are looking at us," Karen protested. "Stop it!" Karen tried to loosen Lauren's hold on her, but couldn't; it was tight.

"I know, and I don't care. Please, please . . . pretty please?" Lauren begged as she continued to hold onto Karen's neck. Karen glanced, as best she could, at other tables. People continued to stare. Karen thought about how ridiculous they must have looked to other diners: ridiculous! She laughed.

"Okay . . . Okay!" Karen said as she laughed again. "Now let me go, and go back to your side of the table so we can get back to eating."

"Thank you, Karen," Lauren said as she released her grip. She kissed Karen's cheek and rested her head back on Karen's. "Now I'll go back. You don't know what this means to Danny—and to me."

"No, I don't, Karen said, still laughing, but I know what it means to me to get you back on your side of the table." Lauren smiled. She moved her head from Karen's and returned to her side of the booth. Having made it over that immense hurdle, the ladies went back to eating and conversing.

* * *

It was Saturday, the day for the dinner. Lauren had looked forward to the day while Karen dreaded it. She had agreed to the dinner, but later regretted it. She had wanted to back out, but Lauren seemed so eager to have her over that Karen didn't want to disappoint her. She was doing it for Lauren, not for Danny.

Lauren had called Karen twice to confirm that she was coming to dinner. She had even threatened her, saying she was putting a lot of work into dinner, and if Karen didn't show up, she was going to track her down like a bloodhound—no, worse than a bloodhound, more like a drug-sniffing police dog. Karen assured Lauren she'd be there, if for no other reason than to avoid being tracked down and eventually caught.

Karen was ten minutes late. But by her standards, she was early, because she wasn't looking forward to having dinner with Danny, and she didn't want to rush it. When she used to attend family gatherings, she was usually close to an hour late. Lauren was peeking out the window when Karen pulled up; she had been checking every couple of minutes.

With Danny at her side, Lauren greeted Karen with a hug. Danny took a step towards Karen; she took two steps away from him. He got the message. Danny put his hands in his pants' pockets and shifted his weight back and forth from his heels to his toes. Karen scanned the area to see if anyone else was there. All was clear. Danny tilted his head and motioned for them to go deeper into the house.

"Lauren, why don't you show Karen around," he said.

"Not now, honey. The food is ready. If Karen wants, I'll show her later." Lauren looked at Karen for agreement. "Okay?" she asked. Karen nodded, but said nothing. Lauren directed Karen to the dining room. Danny followed.

Conversation at dinner was slow at first. It seemed as though it was going to be a conversation between the ladies—and they had a lot to talk about—but Lauren included Danny. She knew which topics were of interest to Danny and Karen—and were safe. Danny allowed Lauren to lead the conversation, and he wisely followed; he did not bring up family or family matters. The three enjoyed a movie together, and later, Karen accepted a tour of the house.

At the end of the visit, Danny and Lauren walked Karen to her car, which was parked in front of the house. Lauren hugged Karen. Karen gave Danny a look, folded her arms and stiffened her body. The message was clear: she and Danny were not on that level. Just because they watched a movie and ate together did not mean they were best friends—or friends at all; that had to be earned. He was not to go near her. Danny understood, and he didn't mind. He smiled and acknowledged her message with a nod. Having Karen at his house eating, and actually talking to him was a major accomplishment. He was pleased with that; it gave him something to build on, and he made it his resolve to do that.

Chapter Eleven

As Frances' health improved and she regained her strength, she felt it was time to return to her own house and no longer be a burden to her children. That meant moving out of Helen's house. She was cautious when bringing up the topic to Helen, because Helen had already let her know that she didn't think it was a good idea for Frances to live alone anymore. She wanted Frances to sell or rent out her house and continue to live with her and her family. Frances would not hear of it.

The topic came up during one of Karen's visits. By this time, Karen no longer went in the house to visit Frances; instead, she would pick Frances up so they could do things together—go places—or she would take Frances home with her for a visit. Karen would walk up to the porch, ring the doorbell, and when Helen opened the door, step just inside the door to escort Frances to her car. On this particular occasion, Helen met Karen at the door. Karen was just about to ring the doorbell when Helen yanked the door open.

"Did you know that mom wants to move back home?" Helen asked without as much as a hello. Karen didn't know what to make of the question. Was Helen trying to suggest that Karen was in on her mother's plan to move out of her house? Frances hadn't mentioned it to Karen, so that was the first Karen had heard of it. Karen didn't like the manner in which the question was asked; she took it personal. And she wasn't going to stand for it.

"No, I didn't, and why would you think I did?" she yelled.

"I didn't say you did, Karen. I asked IF you knew." Karen tilted her head back and threw her nose up in the air.

"And I'm telling you I didn't . . . so get off my back!"

Helen pointed her finger and jabbed the air with it as she shouted, "If you would just listen to me . . ." Frances had heard the noise and raced to the door alongside Helen.

"Girls, girls," Frances cut in. Brad heard the commotion all the way in the kitchen. He darted out of the kitchen toward the noise and burst into the room with the women.

"What's going on here," he demanded. Everyone became silent. He looked from one to the other, waiting for an answer.

"Nothing's going on," Karen said, as she rolled her eyes at Helen. "Nothing at all. I came to pick up mother, and if we don't leave now, we'll miss the beginning of the show." Helen sighed and looked at Brad for support. Brad shrugged his shoulders. Without any knowledge of what was going on, he didn't know what to say or do, and he was not one to get involved in their family tiffs anyway. She knew that, and did not insist.

"Then I guess you should go," Brad said slightly annoyed. Helen looked away.

"I'll see you later, dear," Frances said to Helen as she approached her and kissed her on the cheek.

"Yes," Helen replied as she glared at Karen.

"And we'll talk later, Frances added." Frances then kissed Brad.

"See you later," Karen called out to Helen and Brad as if singing.

"Later," Brad said, still trying to figure out what was going on. Helen said nothing.

Karen whisked Frances to the car, opened and closed the door for her and raced around to the driver's side. She yanked her door open, took a deep breath and exhaled as she plopped in the car. Karen put her back against the car door and faced Frances.

"Mother, what's going on here? What's this about your moving out of Helen's and going back to the house? You can't do that!" Frances snapped her head around to face Karen and looked at her square in the eyes. Frances felt strongly about her decision and wasn't about to back down. She spoke with conviction to get her point across.

"And why not?"

"Because you can't."

"And I asked, why not? I get around fine; I feel fine. I can take care of myself. I have neighbors who look out for each other. Culver City is a fine area; I've lived in that house for over 35 years. And I know most of my neighbors—including the children. I won't be alone or lonely, especially if my children visit regularly. So, what is there to worry about? And besides . . . I don't want to be a burden to my children."

"A burden? I think it's still too early for you to be on your own. I hate to agree with Helen—I really do, mother, but I don't think it's a good idea." Karen closed her eyes and rubbed her temples. "Why don't you spend some time with each of us? Maybe then you won't feel like you're a burden on any one person?"

"What, so I can be a burden to everyone? No, I made up my mind. It's time for me to go home. I don't want to discuss it any more, dear," Frances pleaded. She patted Karen's knee. "Why don't we just enjoy our afternoon together and don't let this ruin it. Okay?" Karen frowned. Karen's expression made it clear that, in her mind, the conversation was not over. "Karen, we can talk about this another time, but not now."

Frances turned her body and then her head to face forward. She folded her hands in her lap and looked straight ahead, fixing her eyes on the road. Silence.

"Okay. Okay," Karen moaned. "We'll talk later." She could tell she wasn't going to get anywhere with her mother at that time, so she figured if she waited until a more convenient time, she might be able to talk some sense into her. Later would be better. But later did not come.

Whenever Karen tried to bring it up, Frances dismissed it. And later, when Helen brought the move up again, Karen pretended to agree with Frances to spite Helen. She told Helen that their mother was, in her opinion, a sane person with all her mental faculties, and therefore had the right to decide where she wanted to stay, and for how long. And if their mother wanted to be on her own and live by herself, her children should respect that.

Helen, in turn, informed Karen that she was going to consult with Danny and Brigit to get their opinions, because she didn't feel that Karen was taking into consideration their mother's age and health.

Karen told Helen that she could do whatever she wanted, but she had to remember that their mother was an adult and was entitled to make her own decisions. And besides, she was neither bedridden nor disabled, and could realistically care for herself.

On that note, Karen stormed out of Helen's house, appearing agitated, but she secretly hoped that the three would override their mother's decision. But they couldn't. Frances would not back down; she was determined to move back home. And the time arrived when Frances did move back into her house—alone.

Karen's apprehension about her mother's moving on her own proved to be unwarranted, and it actually turned out for the better: Karen was able to stop by whenever she wanted without having to make arrangements with Helen. So, she ended up seeing her more often—and she didn't have to see Helen. There were some occasions when Frances wasn't home because she was with one of the other children, but most of the time, Karen stopped by at the right time and was able to visit with her for a while.

If Karen saw either Helen's or Brigit's car outside the house, she would not visit—she'd drive by. But if Danny was there, she would stop by for a short visit. By that time, Karen and Danny had repaired their relationship and were comfortable conversing with each other. That was not the case, however, with her and the girls.

On one occasion, Brigit stopped by while Karen was visiting Frances. Karen excused herself and started to leave, but Brigit wouldn't hear of it. She begged Karen to stay.

"No," Karen said. "I was about to leave anyway, and now you can have mother all to yourself." Brigit's eyes got big. She searched Karen's face. The blank expression on Karen's face made it impossible to read. And her tone matched her face: expressionless.

"I don't know what you mean. I'm willing to share, Karen. So why don't you stay and we can both be with mom." Karen and Brigit stared at each other; Frances stared at the two. Karen gave a little chuckle.

"And I'm going to share her with you, Brigit. I've been here for, oh, over an hour, and now I'm going to share her with you by letting you have some of her time." With that, Karen headed for the door. Brigit rushed on Karen and touched her elbow. Karen paused but continued to look straight ahead; she refused to look at Brigit.

"Please stay," Birgit begged. "We can watch a movie or just talk." Karen moved her elbow from Brigit's touch.

"We have nothing to talk about," Karen blurted out. "Nothing at all . . . and I'm not interested in watching a movie." Karen glanced back at Frances, and noticed that she was opening her mouth to say something. She knew her mother was going to try to insist that they work it out, and Karen didn't want to hear it. She intercepted the comment. She turned her head to face Brigit.

"Maybe another time, but not now. I can't. I just can't," Karen told Brigit. She didn't explain why she couldn't; she just stated that she couldn't. She then gave Brigit a half smile and left. With the opportunity for her line of argument destroyed, before even being presented, Frances closed her mouth and watched Karen leave. Karen's exit was quick; she wanted to avoid any persuasive tactic Brigit might try to use, and any line of argument Frances might add—neither of which would work. She wanted to be left alone.

Chapter Twelve

"Now what?" Karen asked herself out loud. It was 10:30 in the evening, she was in bed about to go into a deep, satisfying sleep, and the phone rang. She hated being disturbed while in bed. She hated it even more than a phone call or personal visit while in the shower. Those she could ignore, but it's difficult to ignore a ringing phone when you're trying to sleep, and even worse once you've been awakened. She rolled over to get closer to the phone on the nightstand and looked at the caller ID: it was Danny's number. Puzzled, she snatched the phone up, wondering why he or Lauren would call at that hour.

"Yes?" she answered. It was Danny.

"Is Lauren there," he asked. Karen jolted up; her breathing quickened.

"No, she left at nine. She should've been home by 9:30—at the latest. And she's not home yet?"

"No," Danny answered. There was a long pause. Karen could sense his anxiety in the way he said 'no'. Karen broke the silence by suggesting that Danny call Lauren on her cell.

"I can't," he answered with obvious concern. "She forgot it. It's here on the table." Karen jumped out of bed, still holding the phone, and began pacing.

"Maybe she stopped at the grocery store on her way home," Karen said. Silence.

"I don't think so, Karen. She went shopping earlier. I think I'd better drive around and see if I can find her. I'll follow her usual route."

"Danny . . ." Karen said, her voice now shaking. "I'll do the same." Karen threw some sweats on and was out the door within five minutes. All sorts of things raced through Karen's mind as she looked for Lauren: an accident, carjacking, or that the car broke down. She hoped, if anything, the car had broken down.

The distance between West Hollywood, where Karen lived, and West L.A., where Danny and Lauren lived, wasn't that far—just a little over seven miles. But travel was through city streets; there was no shortcut by freeway.

About three miles along the way, Karen saw Lauren's car parked on a dimly lit street in a residential neighborhood in Beverly Hills. She pulled up next to Lauren's car. Lauren was sitting behind the wheel with her head down. Karen tapped her horn once to get Lauren's attention. Lauren didn't respond. She tapped again; Lauren raised her head to see the purpose of the horn blowing, and to her relief, discovered Karen, in her car, next to her. Karen pointed down the street, indicating that she was going to park up ahead. Lauren gave a weak smile and nodded. Lauren jumped out of her car and headed for Karen. She was standing on the curb next to Karen's car by the time Karen had parked. They embraced.

"Are you okay?" Karen asked as she scanned Lauren for any visible signs of injury. Lauren nodded.

"I'm glad you're here; I didn't know what to do," Lauren said. "I had a flat, and I forgot my cell phone." She trembled. The evening air was chilly, and she was thinking about her ordeal of being stranded in an unfamiliar area.

"Here," Karen said, handing Lauren her cell phone. "Call Danny on his cell. He's worried sick about you." Lauren took the phone and called Danny. Karen overheard Lauren assure Danny that she was fine. She had a flat, was able to park, but didn't know where to go to use a phone. She didn't want to walk alone on the dark street, so she stayed in the car. She gave Danny their location.

Lauren was still on the phone with Danny when he drove up and parked on the other side of the street. He shoved his phone in his pants' pocket as he got out of the car. He ran across the street to Lauren, held her face in his hands and devoured her mouth, kissing her over and over again.

"I was so worried about you," he said.

"I'm okay," she assured him. Tears trickled down her face.

He pulled Lauren close and held on to her the way a toddler does his favorite toy. He closed his eyes. Karen looked away. This was a very private moment, and she felt like she was intruding.

"Karen," she heard Danny call out. She looked at Danny. "Thank you," he said. Lauren nodded in agreement. Danny removed his left arm from around Lauren and opened it, inviting Karen to come in. She did. He embraced the two women.

"Look . . ." he said, "it's late. We can leave the car here overnight and I'll see about getting the tire fixed first thing in the morning. Karen, do you want us to follow you home?" Karen declined the offer, saying she would be okay. But after that ordeal, Danny wasn't willing to take any chances. He insisted on following her home and made sure she got inside safely. Afterwards, Danny kissed Lauren again and drove off.

Chapter Thirteen

"Jerry stopped by earlier," Ana called out to Karen before Karen had fully entered the gallery. Ana was alone; it was a slow day. She had been browsing through magazines behind the counter when Karen arrived. She stopped browsing, stepped in front of the counter, and focused all of her attention on Karen.

"Thanks, Ana. I'm . . . sorry I missed him," Karen said in a monotone, without a trace of regret or sincerity in her voice. Ana threw her hands up in the air, then dropped them to her side and slapped herself on the thighs.

"Really?" Ana asked. "Are you really sorry you missed him?" Karen nodded and gave Ana a puzzled look, unsure of what Ana was implying. Ana didn't leave any doubt. "I'm asking if you're really sorry, Karen, because I saw you drive by while he was here." She walked toward Karen, pointing at her.

"You had to have seen his car, so why did you keep going? Why didn't you come in, Karen? I thought you two were tight." Ana used the expression 'tight', but she knew that Karen and Jerry were going together. They were a couple. Karen walked past Ana to the counter. She turned to face Ana, leaned on the counter and sighed. Ana stepped in closer to her.

"We are. I care about Jerry—you know that," Karen said.

"Then why'd you do it? Why . . . ?"

"Because I had mother in the car. We had just had lunch and I was going to stop by, but I, um, uh . . . I saw Jerry's car." Karen's shoulders dropped.

"So what?" Ana tried to put the pieces together in her head, but some pieces were missing; the puzzle wasn't complete. Her eyes got big. "Dios mío! Jerry hasn't met your mom yet? Is that what this is about?"

Karen frowned, nodded, then shook her head. "Yes . . . no," she replied, now avoiding eye contact. Ana got in her face and tried to get Karen to look at her.

"Are you saying you don't want your mom to meet Jerry?"

Karen looked at her square in the face. "Yes, that's what I'm saying."

Ana stared at Karen in disbelief and shook her head. "I don't understand you, Karen. You should *want* your mom to meet him. He's not just some guy you're going out with, girl: he's special. Or I thought he was. Have you met his parents, because I don't remember you mentioning it?"

"Yes, and I didn't mention it. It didn't mean anything. I don't want you to jump to any conclusions."

Jerry had been eager for Karen to meet his parents. They traveled a lot, so he made arrangements so they could meet Karen between trips. They had Karen over to their home for an elegant dinner. They liked her, and she liked them. She now understood why Jerry was the way he was: they were genuine, down-to-earth people—who happened to be rich.

"Hasn't he asked to meet your mom?"

" . . . Yes."

"Well . . . what did you say?"

"I told him that he will meet her . . . some day." Ana shook her head and walked away. After a few steps, she turned around and faced Karen.

"My parents meet my boyfriends on the second date. What's the big deal?" Karen shrugged her shoulders. She had asked herself the same question and couldn't explain it.

"He met part of the family; he met Danny. That's enough," Karen said. Karen giggled. "Of course, I have to admit that that was Lauren's doing. She met him at the gallery one day—and insisted he go over to their place for dinner." Karen giggled again. Ana shook her head.

"Don't worry," Karen assured Ana. "He'll meet mother too. Just not now. Not now."

"Then . . . when?" Karen shrugged her shoulders.

"I don't know. I'll know when the time is right, and then I'll do it." Ana gave Karen a look.

"I can see I'm wasting my time with you," Ana said, as she walked away from Karen and returned to browsing magazines behind the counter. "Just wasting my time," she repeated.

* * *

The phone rang. Karen slid the toothbrush from her mouth and spit a glob of minty, light green foam into the bathroom sink.

"I'll get it," she called out to Jerry. She dropped the toothbrush onto the bathroom vanity, swiped her mouth with a towel and raced into the bedroom. Still in bed, Jerry had rolled onto his side to face the phone. He yawned. He wasn't going to answer it; he never did. It was her phone, in her house.

Karen snatched the phone off the hook. It was Helen. Frances had breakfast with the family that morning and mentioned that she was spending the rest of the day with Karen. Helen and the family were going to the L.A. Zoo, so Helen figured she'd offer to drop Frances off at Karen's house rather than have Karen travel to Culver City to pick her up. Jerry overheard Karen say that she was just about to leave the house and preferred that Helen take Frances back home; she would pick her up from there. Karen told Helen that she wouldn't be very long. Karen got off the phone with Helen and headed back to the bathroom.

"What was that about?" Jerry called out. Karen stopped, turned around and gave him a sheepish grin.

"Oh . . . it was Helen. Mother is with them, and I'm supposed to pick her up in a little while. Helen and her family have plans, so Helen's dropping mother off at home, and I have to pick her up there."

"I'll go with you." Jerry raised himself on his elbows and started to get up.

"No," Karen insisted. "I'd rather go alone."

"Okay. Then I'll be dressed when you get back." Jerry sat up. Karen clasped her hands together.

"I'm not bringing her here; we're going out."

"Come here," he said. Karen inched over next to the bed.

Jerry motioned with his finger for her to come closer. She bent over and put her face close to his, awaiting her scolding. He gently lifted her chin and kissed her on the lips. Karen stood upright and squinted her eyes at him.

"Eventually, your mom and I will have to meet. You can't keep avoiding it," he whispered.

"What makes you think I'm avoiding it?" she said, trying to look as shocked and hurt as possible. Instead, her expression was more like that of a cat when car lights beam on them: stunned, with nowhere to hide. She waited for him to answer, but hoped he wouldn't. She had been exposed.

"Because I haven't met your mother yet, and you keep coming up with excuses, Karen—excuses as to why it's not a good time."

Karen wasn't going to admit to anything, so she quickly decided to prove him wrong.

"You're wrong," she protested. "And I'll prove it. Mother and I are going shopping this morning; you can meet us afterwards for lunch. Okay?" Jerry raised one eyebrow and stared at her.

"What?" she asked. She shrugged her shoulders and looked to her right and then left side, as if she were seeking confirmation from some unseen people next to her.

"Nothing. Just call me on my cell and I'll meet you two." He gave her another look. "I'll be waiting." Karen stood there, looking helpless, not knowing what to say. "If you're going to pick her up, you'd better get going," he said. Jerry gave her a little nudge.

"I'm going to call you, Jerry," she promised. The look of guilt was plastered all over her face; she was going to have to follow through.

"Okay, now go ahead. I'm not ready to get up yet anyway," he said. He lay back down and pulled the sheet over his face.

Karen sprang the news on Frances while shopping that they were going to have lunch with Jerry. She tried to figure out the best way to bring it up since she had never mentioned anything about Jerry to Frances before; Frances didn't even know he existed.

"There's this, uh, guy I've been going out with who wants to meet you, mother. I told him that he could join us today for lunch so he can meet you—that is if you don't mind." She hoped her mom would mind. Hoped she would think that she wasn't prepared to meet anyone, that perhaps she didn't look the way she wanted to when meeting someone for the first time.

"A young man . . . , " Frances said, her voice bursting with enthusiasm, "wants to meet me? You've been dating him? How long? What's his name? How did you meet him? Where does . . ."

"Mother . . . stop! I just want you to meet him." Karen took a deep breath. She thought, in retrospect, that it probably wasn't a good idea having Jerry meet her mother after all, but the seed had been planted, and it took root fast.

"I understand that, but there isn't any harm in finding out a little information about him . . . is it, dear?"

"For what purpose, mother?" We've been dating a few months and he asked to meet you. That's it." Karen wasn't being completely honest, because she and Jerry had been dating longer than "a few months"; it had been almost nine months, and they were a couple.

"So, what you're saying, dear, is that introducing us wasn't your idea at all?"

"No, it wasn't. It's not a big deal, mother, and please don't make it into one." Karen took a couple of deep breaths and rubbed her temples. Frances motioned with her hands for Karen to calm down.

"Okay . . . okay, dear. I get it. I'll meet the young man and I won't make it into anything. I'm just meeting a man you're going out with . . . nothing more."

"Thank you," Karen said with a huge sigh of relief. Karen called Jerry and told him where to meet them. "Jerry said he'll be here in twenty minutes. He's rarely late, so we can count on that. If you want to quickly go in another store, we can, or we can wait outside the restaurant. Depending on the wait-time for a seat, we can put our names on the list before he comes. What do you want to do, mother?"

"Let's sit outside the restaurant and wait," Frances answered.

"Okay, let's do that." The women headed toward the

restaurant. Curiosity was killing Frances. She had to hold back from exploding with excitement. She wanted to ask more questions but recognized that that wouldn't be wise. The best thing for her to do was to wait until she could meet the young man in person: that would answer some of them. So Frances avoided asking any further questions about Jerry, and Karen silently prayed that she wouldn't.

The wait at the restaurant was 25-30 minutes; Karen put their names on the list to be seated. They sat outside the restaurant and waited. While they did, Frances kept Karen occupied with talking about how busy the mall was, how busy the restaurant looked, how quickly people were entering and exiting it, and how pleasant the weather was, while she secretly tried to guess which man—of the many men walking in their direction—was Jerry.

Twenty minutes later, Jerry walked up. There had been a couple of men who passed by that Frances thought might have been Jerry, but when he did arrive, she had a deep feeling that it was him. Frances and Jerry were excited to meet each other, and they greeted one another as though they were long-lost relatives—without embracing. They shook hands and didn't let go. They studied each other's face and all-over appearance. They quickly bonded.

"I've been asking Karen for months to meet you," Jerry said.

"Oh? Months, you say?" Frances said with genuine surprise as she glanced at Karen to see the expression on her face. Karen in turn gave Jerry a look of disapproval. It didn't faze him, though; he acted as though he were oblivious to her stare.

"Well . . . I did," he continued. He gave Karen a look. Karen didn't offer an explanation or apology. She gave a loud sigh and rolled her eyes at Frances and then at Jerry. Neither one let her look of disapproval dampen their enthusiasm in meeting each other.

"And now you've met," Karen said with some sarcasm. "And life goes on," she continued. Frances and Jerry hit if off right away. When they were finished eating, Frances and Jerry were talking about seeing each other again, while Karen smiled and neither confirmed nor denied future plans for them to get together. In Jerry's mind, there was no doubt that he would see

Frances again: he and Karen were a couple—almost family.

Frances wasn't sure as to how serious their relationship was, but her enthusiasm indicated that she hoped it was very serious. And since she hadn't met any of Karen's previous boyfriends, she assumed that he must be, at least, someone special. Before Jerry left, he and Frances hugged each other and promised to see each other again. Karen remained silent.

"I like Jerry," Frances said as they headed toward another store, after Jerry left. "He's a very charming young man. I hope to see a lot of him." Frances eyed Karen for confirmation. Karen was in deep thought. She did not hear Frances; she did not respond. She was looking far off into space, thinking about nothing in particular.

"Karen?" Frances called out. "Are you listening to me? I said I hope to see a lot of Jerry."

"Jerry? Oh, Jerry . . . yes, you want to see him again. I hear you, mother. Why don't we call it a day and go in? I think we've both had enough excitement for the day. I know I have." Frances looked at Karen, puzzled, but dared not ask again about Jerry—or bring up his name. She sensed that that was not the time for any type of discussion. She sensed that something was not quite right.

"Yes," Frances agreed, "let's go home." Frances didn't want to jeopardize her chance of seeing Jerry again, so she remained silent. She figured that since it took so long for Karen to introduce them in the first place, it might take her a while to invite him over again if she wasn't happy with the outcome of their meeting. But it was too late: the damage had been done.

Chapter Fourteen

"Are you coming to the family reunion, slash, barbecue next month?" Danny asked Karen one evening when she went to visit him and Lauren.

"I don't know. I haven't really thought about it. I'm certainly not going to rearrange my schedule for it. I'll see if I'm available then." Karen hadn't gotten settled yet in their house; she had just gotten in and was about to sit down.

"No!" Lauren protested. "You've got to come. They've been planning it for months. Put it on your calendar." Karen looked at the two. They were both beaming as though they were up to something and unable to contain themselves. Clearly, something was going on; this was not just a barbecue. Karen remained standing.

"Why, what's going on?" Karen asked. Lauren moved closer to Danny. He put his arm around Lauren's shoulder.

"What . . ?" Karen demanded. Karen was not keen on surprises. She waited for an answer.

"We're going to announce our engagement," Lauren exploded. She pulled her hand out from behind her to flash her engagement ring in front of Karen.

"Ooh, let me see that," Karen said. She held Lauren's hand in hers and examined the ring. She gave Danny a smile of approval. "It's beautiful. Good job, Danny."

"We want you to be there," Lauren said. "No one else knows. Well . . . no one outside of my family. Danny asked my dad yesterday, and of course, dad said, yes."

Lauren's family was very religious. Her parents did not

approve of Lauren and Danny living together without marriage. They refused to visit Danny and Lauren in their "house of sin," but occasionally invited them over for dinner when it was only their immediate family. So, when Danny asked Lauren's father if he could have Lauren's hand in marriage, Lauren's dad was overjoyed. To him, the wedding was long overdue.

Karen opened her arms wide and gave Lauren and Danny a group hug. No longer strangers, Karen felt very comfortable doing it.

"I'm happy for you two," she said. "Okay, I'll be at the family reunion, and I'll even rearrange my schedule, if necessary. I think I remember getting an invitation a while ago, but I didn't really read it. I'll do that when I get home. I think I still have it."

"And . . ." Lauren began. "I have another favor to ask." Lauren put her hands together as if she were praying, but said nothing. Karen looked at Danny for an explanation, but couldn't get eye contact; he was staring at Lauren, beaming with pride. Karen broke the silence.

"What's the favor?" Karen asked. She put her hands on her hips and widened her stance. "What is it?" she demanded. She waited for an answer. She had already agreed to go to the reunion; she couldn't imagine what more they could want from her.

"I was wondering if you would be in my wedding," Lauren asked. Karen's arms dropped to her side. She redistributed her weight on her legs, which at that moment seemed like they were going to give out on her.

"Me? I'm, I'm shocked," she said.

"Don't be," Lauren said. "Just say, yes. My sister is going to be my maid of honor, and I would love it if you would be one of my bridesmaids—I'm having four. Will you?" she begged.

"Sure, I'll be in your wedding. It would be an honor." Lauren grabbed Karen and hugged her tight.

"Thank you, thank you, thank you, Karen. You don't know what this means to me."

"You really don't," Danny interjected. "She's been driving me crazy wondering what you'd say."

"What else could I say," Karen chuckled. "I'm honored and flattered."

"We've become so close," Lauren said. "I consider you to be one of my best friends, and I want you there . . . with me on my wedding day."

Karen was moved. Moved by Lauren's openness and sincerity, Karen hugged Lauren.

"And I consider you to be one of my best friends too. I already think of you as family. Hey . . . I feel closer to you than to either of my sisters. Now . . . see? Soon you really will be family. Before we watch the movie, you've got to tell me how Danny proposed." They settled on the sofa, and Lauren recounted how Danny proposed to her.

Danny had told Lauren that he was taking her out to dinner to celebrate something that happened at work that day. He told her to dress up for the dinner. She thought he had gotten a raise or promotion, and she was excited about it. Lauren dressed up as he had told her. When they were in the restaurant, he pulled out the ring and asked her to marry him.

Danny said Lauren started to cry, and people began staring at them, wondering what had happened.

Lauren explained that she was so choked up she could barely breathe, no less answer him. All she could do was nod, so she nodded—with tears streaming down her face. He put the ring on her finger, went to her side of the table and kissed her. Only then did some concerned people resume eating their meal; some clapped. Lauren said she was completely surprised by the proposal—surprised and ecstatic. Now she was looking forward to announcing their engagement to the rest of the family. Karen assured them that when they did, she'd be there.

Chapter Fifteen

Frances thought it was a good time to initiate a conversation with Karen about Jerry. She'd asked a number of times how he was doing, and Karen always gave a one-word answer—"fine," or "good," or "okay." Her tone always let Frances know that there would be no further discussion, so Frances didn't pursue it. This time, though, Frances felt adventurous: she was going to demand more information no matter how tight-lipped Karen tried to be. Enough time had passed to where she wondered whether she'd ever see him again. She had to know.

"Karen, I've been wondering about Jerry," she said matter-of-factly. "How is he?"

"He's fine, mother."

"I see . . ." Frances said. "You say, 'fine'. The last time I asked you, you said, 'fine'; you always say he's doing fine. I ask, Karen, because I thought I would have seen him again by now. He seemed to be such a nice young man; I thought he and I were going to become, well . . . close, but I haven't seen him since." There! She said what she had wanted to say. Now, she waited for Karen to explain why she hadn't brought Jerry around for another visit.

Karen didn't offer an explanation. Instead, she shrugged her shoulders and said, "I guess we don't always get what we want, mother. That's the way life is: it's full of disappointments." Karen said this as though they had been engaged in a long conversation and was exhausted, tired of dredging up the same old topic.

"I don't understand, dear. I thought you and Jerry were

dating. I got the impression you had been dating for a while. And frankly, I thought he was perfect for you." Frances thought Karen would appreciate that she had her approval of Jerry as a worthy suitor. Admittedly, Frances had seen Jerry just the one time, but she considered herself a good judge of character, and to her, Jerry was a good person, and therefore, perfect for Karen.

"Well, then I guess you were wrong, mother. And who are you to decide who's perfect for me?" Karen thumped herself on her chest with an open hand. "That's MY decision," Karen lashed out. Frances put her hand in front of her mouth to cover her hanging jaw, but her eyes revealed her shock at Karen's statement: they were twice as large as usual and welled with tears. Frances took a deep breath and spoke calmly.

"Does that mean you and Jerry aren't dating anymore?"

"That's right, mother, it's over; we broke up," Karen said as she wagged her head. Frances shook her head. She let out a big sigh and pointed her finger at Karen.

"Karen, I hope you didn't break up with him because I liked him, or took an interest in him. I did not meddle in your affairs; I did not play matchmaker. I did not choose the young man—you did. All I did was agree with your choice. I'm sorry that you were bothered by that." Frances took another deep breath and shook her head again.

"You don't need to worry, because I will not mention his name again." She closed her eyes and shook her head one last time. She then opened her eyes and gave Karen a half smile. "So, Karen, what did you have in mind for us to do today?" she asked.

Chapter Sixteen

It was one of Karen's and Lauren's movie nights. It was Karen's turn to travel, so she went over to Danny's, and he and Lauren were supposed to supply the DVD. Lauren opened the door to let Karen in; Melissa, Brigit's daughter was by her side.

"I didn't know you had company," Karen said as she eyed Melissa and scanned the area for any sign of Brigit. There was none.

"No, just Melissa," Lauren assured her. Lauren pulled Melissa close to her and put her arm around the little girl's shoulder. "We're babysitting."

"Then you're expecting Brigit. I won't stay." Karen turned to leave. She didn't want to delay and be forced to have any contact with Brigit.

"I don't see why . . . When she picks Melissa up, she usually doesn't come in. Brigit comes to the door for Melissa, I walk Melissa to the door, and then they leave . . . and that's that. Come on." Lauren reached over and tugged at Karen's arm. "Brigit and Michael are having a night out. Come on," Lauren insisted. Karen turned to face the two. Melissa had a puzzled look on her face, no doubt wondering why Karen would go to the house and not come inside, and why she didn't speak to her.

"Okay . . ." Karen said. She then realized that in her haste she did not acknowledge or speak to Melissa. She lowered her eyes to look at Melissa and saw the look on her little face. Karen gave Melissa a big smile as she bent over to hug her. "And how is Miss Melissa tonight?" she asked Melissa.

"Fine," Melissa answered as she wiggled her fingers to wave

hello. The puzzled look was replaced with a shy smile.

"Is Lauren keeping you busy . . . or are you keeping her busy?"

"Me and Aunt Lauren are coloring."

"Excuse me. So, it's *Aunt Lauren*?" Karen said as she winked at Lauren. Lauren nodded and smiled. Melissa ran to the area where they had been coloring, picked up some sheets of paper with samples of her artwork and brought them back to Karen.

"See, I colored these." She handed the pages to Karen. Karen examined the drawings as they headed to the living room.

"Very nice," Karen said. Maybe we can color for a while too. That is if *Aunt Lauren* doesn't mind." Karen looked at Lauren for approval. Lauren nodded.

"That sounds great," Lauren said. I'll start heating up dinner while you two color. Danny'll be back soon; he went to the store to pick up a few things. We're going to have a lot of fun tonight: We're going to watch a family movie. We don't know which one yet; we're gonna let Melissa pick which one she wants to see. Right, Melissa?" Melissa smiled and nodded.

Karen made her way to the makeshift work area: throw pillows on the floor, by the sofa table, which had crayons and coloring books on it. She settled on one of the pillows. Melissa knelt on a pillow next to Karen and resumed working on her last masterpiece. No longer needed, Lauren left and went to the kitchen.

Later, when Brigit arrived to pick up Melissa, the little girl was sitting on Karen's lap, coloring. They had already finished eating and watching the movie, and had returned to coloring.

"Your mommy's here," Lauren called out to Melissa from the front door. Melissa didn't respond. "I'll get her," Lauren said to Brigit. Lauren headed toward the living room; Brigit followed her.

"Danny, Karen, Melissa . . . Hey," Brigit said as she tilted her head to each one. "I'm here." Karen turned her head toward Brigit, stared at her for a second, frowned, and then went back to looking at the drawing she and Melissa were working on. Brigit did not react to Karen's snubbing her; she acted as if it didn't have any affect on her. But it did, because Brigit was the type of person who wanted everyone to like her. And to have one of her own sisters refuse to even speak to her bothered her tremendously.

"Hey," Danny said.

"Hi, Mommy. I'm coloring with Aunt Karen," Melissa announced.

"I see. It looks like you two are having fun, honey, but it's time to go now. Daddy's waiting in the car."

"But I don't want to go; I want to stay with Aunt Karen."

"This is not Aunt Karen's house; she'll be going home soon too," Brigit said. Karen remained silent. She stopped coloring and turned her head toward Brigit again. She looked at Brigit, or through Brigit, with a blank expression.

"Maybe you can color another day with Aunt Karen," Brigit said as she looked at Karen for some sort of confirmation. Karen rolled her eyes at Brigit and still said nothing.

"Aunt Karen . . ?" Melissa said as she looked over her shoulder to look in Karen's face. "Can I come over your house and color with you?" Karen looked down at Melissa.

"Sure you can," Karen answered with a smile as she hugged Melissa and put her face next to hers. Karen helped Melissa off her lap. "I'll see you soon," Karen said as she smoothed Melissa's hair down on the back of her head.

"Okay," Melissa said. Melissa skipped over to Danny, hugged him and then went over to Lauren and hugged her.

"I'll give you a call so the two of you can get together. Okay?" Brigit said. Karen gave Brigit a blank stare and said nothing. She rolled her eyes and looked away.

"Karen, I'm talking to you."

"And I'm ignoring you," Karen said to herself out loud. When she realized what she had done, and that they had heard what she had said, she looked at Melissa, who was staring at her, and gave her a half smile. "We'll get together soon," Karen said to Melissa." Karen looked in Brigit's general area. "My schedule's been unpredictable lately, so I, uh, I'll call you, Brigit," she said without giving Brigit any eye contact. Brigit's shoulders dropped.

"Okay . . . and we need to talk," Brigit said.

"You think?" Karen said with no emotion. She looked at

Brigit and locked eyes with her. "It's years too late for that," she said just above a whisper. "Years." Brigit thought about responding to Karen's comment and pursuing a conversation to clear things up, but as she had stated, Michael was in the car, and she didn't want to keep him waiting. She threw her hands up in the air, hugged Lauren, grabbed Melissa's hand and left. Dealing with Karen would have to wait until another day.

Chapter Seventeen

The family reunion/barbecue came way too fast for Karen; to her, the month flew by. She didn't look forward to being among a crowd of relatives she never bothered to keep in touch with. But to Danny and Lauren, the wait seemed like forever: they were eager to share their news. And finally, here was the day.

Helen, of course, did most of the organizing for the barbecue. She and her family went to the park early that day to set up the picnic area they had reserved. Brigit and her family, and Danny and Lauren joined them a little later to help out and keep them company.

There was an abundance of food: some of it was purchased from the market already prepared, and some family members volunteered to bring their favorite dishes, plus they had hot dogs, hamburgers, chicken and ribs for the men to barbecue on the grill. Karen offered to bring a sheet cake; Helen accepted the offer. She accepted but didn't count on Karen's taking the cake, because Karen had proven herself to be unreliable. Other relatives had also promised to take cakes, so Helen was sure there would be plenty without Karen's cake.

Karen arrived—with Jerry; he was holding the sheet cake. Karen was shocked to see how many people were there. Even her dad's brother—her Uncle Phillip from Florida—and his family were there. As she scanned the crowd, she saw some relatives she hadn't seen since she was a child but could still recognize. She figured that the others she either had never met or just couldn't remember because they were older and looked different. There were so many of them. Danny and Lauren were the first to greet her and Jerry.

"Where should we put the cake?" Karen asked Lauren. Jerry held the cake up.

"The desserts are over here on this table," Lauren said as she pointed and led them to one of the tables loaded with cakes, pies, cookies and other sweets. Jerry put the cake with the other desserts. His eyes searched through the crowd, focused and locked on someone. Karen followed his line of vision: it was Frances. Frances had seen him too, and was heading in their direction. As she approached, Frances extended her hand to shake Jerry's, but he gave her a light hug. Frances gave Karen a quick hug and returned her attention to Jerry.

"I'm so happy to see you," Frances said to Jerry as she looked at Karen through the corner of her eye. She cautiously avoided acting overly excited at seeing him.

"Yeah, Karen tried to get rid of me, but she eventually came around," he said with a grin. Frances turned to face Karen. She held her breath as she waited for Karen to respond. Karen stared Jerry down for a couple of seconds. Jerry nodded and gave Karen a 'you know it's true' look. Karen smiled, then laughed. She looked at Frances and nodded.

"I hate to admit it, but I did miss him." Jerry reached over and squeezed Karen's hand. Karen had broken up with Jerry, saying their relationship wasn't working out and that she needed space. She asked him not to call her anymore, and he respected her request. He did not call—at all. But they continued to see each other in passing at art trade shows, and Karen missed Jerry. She missed him a lot. She missed him and the special attention he gave her. She missed the conversations they had. And she missed the way he'd look at her when he thought she couldn't see him, but she did. So she swallowed her pride, approached him at one of the shows and asked him if he wanted to go out. Jerry said, yes—without hesitation—and they were a couple again.

"How long has it been since you two started dating again?" Frances asked with controlled excitement. "Because . . . Karen didn't mention it, and we see each other almost every week."

"I know, mother, and I appreciate that you kept your promise and didn't bring him up. I didn't want any pressure; I didn't want to be rushed." Karen glanced at Jerry and then eyed Frances. "And I still don't, mother," she mumbled. Frances had learned her lesson. She had no intention of meddling in their relationship. She gave Karen a slight smile, barely curving the corners of her mouth, to acknowledge that she heard and would comply with Karen's request.

Brigit rushed up on them with Melissa in hand. She had seen this unknown-to-her male person with her family from a distance, and she wanted to know who he was. She could sense he was with Karen. She made her way up to Jerry and stood nearby. She gave him a big smile and waited for an introduction. None was given. Jerry gave Brigit a hello nod and Melissa a warm smile.

"Hi, Melissa," he said, patting Melissa's back.

"Hi," Melissa answered, waving her fingers at him.

"I see you've met my daughter. I'm Brigit, Karen's sister." Brigit extended her hand to Jerry. "And you are . . ?"

"Jerry . . . Jerry Hamilton," he answered as he shook her hand.

Brigit tilted her head and shifted her eyes, back and forth, from Jerry to Karen to indicate she wanted more information, but Karen offered none. Brigit looked at the others, raised her eyebrows and waited. Still, no one offered any information.

"Come, Jerry, let me introduce you to the rest of the family," Frances said. She put her arm around Jerry's, and whisked him away into the crowd of relatives. Since no one was cooperating, Brigit felt she had to be more forceful. She directed her attention to Danny and Lauren since Karen ignored her and Frances took her leave.

"And who is Jerry?" she asked. Danny clapped his hands together.

"I'm, uh, going to help the guys with the barbecuing," he said, pointing in their direction. He stroked Lauren's back and made a quick exit. Lauren smiled and looked in Karen's direction. She didn't think it was her duty to tell Brigit who Jerry was. She waited for Karen to speak up. Brigit turned her attention to Karen again.

"Karen, who is Jerry?" Brigit asked. Brigit felt left out. It seemed like everyone else knew him—even her daughter. That bothered her. She wanted to be in the know too. She was used to being in the know. In school, at work—everywhere, people liked Brigit, and she was included in almost all the goings on, or had knowledge of them. Being left out was a new experience for her, one she couldn't bear.

"He's a friend. What's the big deal?" Karen answered.

"It's not a big deal, Karen. I'm asking because he seems to be your guest—correct me if I'm wrong. He came with you to a family event, and everyone seems to know him: Melissa, Danny, Lauren—and even Mom knows him. That's all. And I've never seen him before. I'm not trying to pry."

"Then don't!" Karen stared at Brigit square in the face and didn't say another word. She didn't think Brigit was entitled to any additional information, and she was not about to offer any.

Brigit looked at Lauren for support, but Lauren was busy trying to keep Melissa occupied with small talk. She didn't want Melissa to sense any conflict between the adults, although it was obvious that an argument was brewing.

"Lauren, will you please take Melissa over with the other children to play? I'll be over in a few minutes. I want to talk to Karen for a second," Brigit pleaded. Lauren nodded.

"Come on, Melissa, let's go play with the other kids," Lauren said. She grabbed Melissa's hand and whisked her away. Brigit then turned her attention back to Karen; she held her breath for a few seconds to maintain her composure.

"Why do you hate me?" Brigit asked while exhaling, her voice breaking up.

"I don't hate you. I don't feel anything towards you," Karen answered.

"Then why do you treat me like that? I've tried over and over to get close to you, and you won't let me. You ignore me like I'm not here. I appreciate your taking time to do things with Melissa, but I'd like us to get along too. If there's something I did in the past to hurt you, I'm sorry."

Karen locked eyes with Brigit.

"You didn't do anything. Okay?"

"Then what is it?"

"It's nothing. Just drop it."

"How can I when you keep ignoring and avoiding me?" Brigit's eyes welled with tears.

Karen thought about it: it really wasn't Brigit's fault that Helen included Brigit in her exclusive group while eliminating her.

"Okay, I'll stop ignoring you," Karen said reluctantly. "Okay?" Karen wanted the conversation to end before it became too involved with details about the past and hurt feelings. Ideally, she wanted Brigit to go away, but she wouldn't.

Brigit stared at Karen; a few tears rolled down Brigit's face. She swiped them off with her fingertips. Brigit didn't want to end the conversation. She wanted to know why Karen avoided her and she wanted to settle it right then while she had Karen in front of her.

"Okay?" Karen asked with a little more force. It was clear that Karen wasn't going to cooperate. Persistence on Brigit's part could lead to a heated argument. Brigit weighed the situation and circumstances, and decided it might not be the right time to pursue the conversation. The family reunion was supposed to be a time for the family to enjoy being together again, seeing some, perhaps, after a long time, and getting a chance to meet others who were new to the family. It was supposed to be a happy occasion. An argument between her and Karen there, at the time, would surely affect other people, and she didn't want that. She didn't want to ruin it for others. So . . . Brigit nodded.

"Okay," Brigit said. Her shoulders dropped; she sighed.

"Jerry is someone I've been going out with for a little while. That's it! Satisfied?" Karen asked. Brigit nodded again. She reached out to hug Karen. She hoped Karen would bend a little in her direction, but Karen didn't budge; she stood still and stiff, as lifeless as a mannequin. Brigit moved closer to Karen and hugged Karen's stiff body and patted her back."

"I'm going to check on Lauren and Melissa," Brigit said as she walked away. "I'll see you later." Karen wrapped her arms around herself and nodded.

"And . . . I guess I'll go over and see what mother has done with Jerry," Karen called out as she walked in the direction to where Frances had taken Jerry.

Jerry was standing around laughing and having a good time with some of the guys when Karen walked up. She and Jerry shared a smile. Karen searched for, and spotted, Frances: she was at one of the tables chatting with some of the older women, including Pamela. Karen gave Jerry a slight wave and went over to join the women; he continued talking with the guys.

When Karen reached the table, Frances broke off her conversation with the ladies for a minute to tell Karen that she was happy to see Jerry again. She then resumed chatting with the other women; Karen joined in.

Later, when the large group was in the middle of eating, Danny pulled out a whistle he had brought for the occasion and proceeded to blow it.

"Hello . . . Can I have your attention everyone?" he yelled. I have an important announcement to make." Some continued talking. Danny gave a couple of more short whistles. "Hello . . . hello, I have an important announcement to make," he yelled again. The crowd slowly quieted down and gave Danny their attention. Danny pulled Lauren, who was a few steps away, closer to him.

"I asked this beautiful woman here to marry me, and she said, yes. Lauren and I are getting married!" Lauren, smiling from ear to ear, held her hand up and waved it from side to side so they could see her beautiful diamond ring. The crowd exploded with applause and cheer. Some may not have known Danny prior to the reunion, or quite how they were related to him, but they knew that they were kin, and they were happy for him.

"Kiss . . . kiss . . . kiss," the crowd chanted. Danny was more than willing to comply with their request by giving Lauren a lengthy, passionate kiss. The group cheered and applauded again. Danny and Lauren's engagement was now public.

Chapter Eighteen

"Lauren . . . someone's at the door," Karen called out from the living room to Lauren in the kitchen. "Are you expecting anybody?"

"No, and I don't know who it could be."

"Do you want me to get it?"

"Could you? I'll be there in a second."

Karen made her way to the door and opened it; Brigit was standing there with a small, white paper bag in her hand. Brigit dangled the bag in front of Karen and smiled; Karen frowned. Brigit ignored the face.

"I thought I'd stop by and visit for a while," Brigit said. I bought some pastries."

"Oh . . . Lauren's in the kitchen," Karen said, as she tilted her head towards the kitchen. She moved slightly to the side to allow Brigit to pass her and proceed to the kitchen. Brigit ignored the gesture.

"I didn't come by just to see Lauren; I came to see you too."

"Me . . . ? How did you know I was here?"

"Mom told me."

"Mother? I should've known," Karen said. ". . . still interfering," she mumbled.

Brigit swung her arm with the pastries over Karen's shoulder and hugged Karen's stiff body. Karen had said she was going to stop ignoring her, and this was her chance to prove it. Brigit was holding her to her word. And Michael had assured Brigit that with her winning personality, it was just a matter of time before she'd win Karen over, just as she did with him. This was her chance to prove Michael true.

"Who is it?" Lauren called out. Karen took a step back and turned to the side, before answering, as if the change in position facilitated throwing her voice into the other room. What it did do was force Brigit to release her hold on her.

"It's Brigit," she answered. Karen gave Brigit a weak smile. Lauren entered the room with two ice-blended drinks. She was sipping on one. "Hey . . . What's up?" Lauren asked Brigit.

"Nothing," Brigit answered. "I just stopped by for a visit." Lauren could feel Karen's stare of disapproval. She glanced in Karen's direction and then back at Brigit with a smile.

"Good," Lauren said. "Then I guess I'll have to make another drink." Lauren smiled at Karen and led them into the living room. She handed Karen the second drink and set her own on a table. "Have a seat," Lauren said to Brigit. Brigit handed Lauren the bag of pastries and plopped down onto the sofa. Lauren peeked in the bag. "Ooh . . . yummy! These look good. We can eat them a little later. I'll put them in the kitchen."

"Don't you have a family?" Karen asked Brigit with a dead-pan face and no emotions in her voice. Lauren gave Karen a look. Brigit didn't respond to the comment or allow it to affect her enthusiasm in being there.

"Michael went over to Helen's with the guys to see the game, and Melissa's with mom; she has the boys, and I'm all alone. So . . . here I am."

"Yes, here you are," Karen repeated, rolling her eyes. Lauren gave Karen another look and shook her head at her.

"I'm glad you came," Lauren said. "Karen and I are looking through bridal catalogs. You can help too. We're basically just hanging out. "Karen, why don't you give Brigit a catalog while I put the pastries up and fix another drink? Brig, do you like strawberry daiquiris, 'cause that's what we're having, and I'm pretty good at making them?"

"Sure," Brigit said with the enthusiasm of a schoolgirl just allowed in an exclusive circle. "I'd love one." Lauren left to prepare the drink. Brigit smiled at Karen and waited. Karen grabbed one of the catalogs spread out on the living room table and handed it to Brigit.

"Here, you can look through this one." Karen sat on the other end of the sofa and started looking through another catalog. Brigit flipped through the pages and quickly found a dress that she thought would be perfect for Lauren. She pointed it out to Karen. Karen inched closer to Brigit.

"No, I don't think that would work," Karen said. "See the high waist? It would detract from Lauren's small waist. She needs something more tailored like . . . (Karen flipped through some pages until she found an example of what she meant.) "This!" she said pointing at a dress. Brigit nodded and listened to Karen explain other features Lauren's dress should have. Brigit and Karen went back and forth on a few more gowns until Lauren joined them with Brigit's drink in hand. Then the three scoured through the magazines together for the perfect wedding dress for Lauren.

Admittedly, Karen and Brigit didn't become close with this one visit, but they did reach the point to where they began talking and listening to each other. For maybe the first time since grade school, they were communicating with each other.

* * *

Karen didn't waste any time in bringing up Brigit's surprise visit and her disapproval to Frances—the perpetrator. The fact that the visit had positive results did not matter to Karen; she made her own surprise visit on Frances. She first spent a little time on small talk, and then—she let Frances have it.

"Brigit stopped by Lauren's yesterday while I was there," Karen said.

"Yes, I know, dear." Frances nodded and smiled. She was pleased that—in her opinion—her girls were patching up their differences and that she, in some small way, had contributed to it. She expected Karen to tell her about the great time they had together and to thank her for making it happen. She knew they had a good time, because Brigit had told her about it.

"Mother, you have to stop meddling in my life," Karen said. The smile disappeared from Frances' face. It was replaced by a hanging jaw and flashbulb-struck eyes.

"Meddling . . . how?" Frances asked.

"Oh, come now, mother. I know you told Brigit I was there."

"That's right; I didn't think it was a secret. She said she had a good time."

"That's not the point, mother. You've got to stop trying to manipulate people. At least stop trying to control . . . me. If the others don't mind, that's up to them, but I don't like it, mother, and I'm asking you nicely to stop."

Frances sighed. She thought she had done a good thing. To learn that Karen felt otherwise came as a complete shock. If Karen wanted to make her feel guilty, her plan failed. Frances refused to have any guilt feelings, especially since it turned out for the best.

"I don't call it manipulating people if a mother wants her children to get along with each other and tries to help them get on the right track." Karen took a deep breath.

"You're wrong, mother. Sometimes you just have to let things be as they are. Everything can't be the way you'd like. You have to accept that. If you try to do the same thing with Helen . . ." Karen opened her eyes wide, glared at Frances and shook her head. "I'll never forgive you. Do you understand, mother?" she asked through gritted teeth, her eyes bulging.

"But . . ."

"No, mother! That's where I draw the line. And I'm letting you know now so it won't come as a surprise. You decide."

"Okay . . . Okay," Frances relented. Frances shook her head. "I won't . . ." Frances took a deep breath. "get involved with whatever's going on between you and Helen."

"Thank you." That was all Karen wanted to hear. She felt she had gotten her point across to Frances; she had accomplished her goal. She could now leave. "Then, I guess I'd better go," she said. "Jerry's waiting for me. He sends his love." Frances gave a faint smile.

"Give him a kiss for me, will you, dear?"

"Sure. And he sent you one. Here . . ." Karen kissed Frances on the cheek, said good-bye, and left.

It was easy for Frances to keep her promise regarding not becoming involved with Karen's and Helen's relationship with each other, because Helen didn't want anything to do with Karen either. Helen and Karen barely tolerated each other. It was obvious they didn't like to be around each other: their conversations were formal and very brief. If they could get by with just a 'hello', they would. They made sure to keep their distance from each other, even when in the same room.

Neither Karen nor Helen wanted Helen's boys to miss out on having a relationship with their Aunt Karen, so Karen invited the boys over for outings with her and Jerry, and Helen, in turn, allowed them to go. And the boys always had a great time. The two sisters cooperated on matters involving the family, but otherwise had nothing whatsoever to do with each other. It seemed as though their differences would last forever.

Chapter Nineteen

Their special day finally arrived: Danny and Lauren's wedding. Lauren was on time. There was no way she was going to delay her getting married to the man of her dreams. And Danny was way early. He was eager to marry the woman he believed to be his soul mate.

The small church was filled to capacity with family and friends from both sides—Danny's and Lauren's. Lauren's parents were bursting with pride. All was forgiven for Danny and Lauren having lived together in sin and shaming them; that was in the past, forgotten. They were given a brand new slate.

Lauren's parents invited friends from their church to witness the union of their daughter in holy matrimony. They wanted everyone to know that their daughter's relationship with Danny was honorable and had God's blessing, so they made sure to invite the two biggest gossipers from their church to ensure that the word would spread to everyone—and fast. They even requested that seats be reserved for them close to the section reserved for the family. Lauren's parents did this even though they did not truly consider the two women to be in their circle of friends.

On her way to the room reserved for the bridal party in the church, Lauren's cell phone rang. It was one of the band members hired to play at the reception. There had been a terrible accident on the freeway that caused the closure of all lanes. He called to inform Lauren that they were not going to be able to make it to the reception. They were stuck on the freeway and couldn't get off. With that news, Lauren started to fall apart. She began trembling and sobbing. In her mind, her special day was ruined. Karen rushed over to her side to find out what had happened. People gathered around them, inquiring as to what the problem was.

Helen noticed the commotion and flew over. She stepped in and immediately took charge. Before hearing anything, she assured people that Lauren had wedding-day jitters and that everything would be fine. She encouraged them to find their seats and enjoy the wedding. She then directed Lauren and Karen to a private area where they could talk further. She dabbed Lauren's face with some tissue she had brought for herself for when Danny and Lauren exchanged their vows, and handed Lauren a few.

"Lauren . . . Lauren, it's going to be okay. Everything's going to be fine," she assured Lauren without knowing what was going on. "Now, tell me what happened. What's the problem?" Lauren began wringing her hands together and repeated what the band member had told her. Listening on, Karen began to unravel. She tried to hold back the tears but couldn't.

"First of all, why did they call you?" Helen questioned. "That's ridiculous! You don't have time to worry about such things: that's something your wedding planner should handle. They should have called her or him; they never should have called you." She waited for an answer from Lauren. Lauren was silent. "You did hire a wedding planner—didn't you?" Lauren shook her head.

"Who doesn't use a wedding planner nowadays?" Helen asked in disbelief.

"I wanted to make sure everything was done exactly right—the way I wanted. And now look!" Lauren put her face in her cupped hands and began to sob again.

"I'm sorry. I shouldn't have said that," Helen said. "But it's fixable, Lauren. Don't worry about it. It will be fixed. I'll take care of it personally." Helen released Lauren's hands, held Lauren's chin in her hand and made Lauren look in her eyes.

"Look at me," she said. "It will be fixed. So, go in there now with the rest of your bridal party and get yourself together." She gave Lauren a once-over look. "You look beautiful," she said. "And we don't want to spoil it with tears. Enjoy your day, Lauren, because everything will be fine. Don't let anything ruin your day. Okay?" Lauren sniffled a couple of times, nodded and dragged a tissue across her face.

"Thank you," Lauren said. Helen hugged Lauren.

"Yes . . . thank you," Karen agreed.

"We're family," Helen said to Karen. "We're supposed to be there for each other." Karen gave Helen a half nod. She didn't know if Helen's statement was a personal attack on her, or if Helen was simply stating a truth, but Karen understood the logic and agreed: family should be there for each other.

Helen then asked Lauren what style of music the band was supposed to play at the reception and the key songs she had requested, such as the song she and the wedding party were going to enter the reception to, the song she and Danny were going to dance to, and the song she and her father were going to dance to. Lauren gave Helen the information. After soliciting help from a few family members, Helen left the boys under Brad's charge and left the church to accomplish her mission.

Helen had a way of talking to people that made them have complete confidence in her and her ability to make things happen. Lauren no longer worried about the reception and the music—and whether they would come together. She was a beautiful, graceful princess in a royal procession leading to her handsome prince. The townsfolk marveled at her beauty as she waltzed up the aisle to be at his side. They took pictures and applauded. Her prince was captivated by her beauty. Danny's smile told of his love for Lauren even before their vows were spoken.

The marriage ceremony proceeded as planned and rehearsed; it was perfect. Lauren was happy, Danny was pleased, and Lauren's parents were ecstatic. The tears shed were those of joy as friends and relatives witnessed the couple's promise to love each other for the rest of their lives.

After the wedding, the bridal party remained in the church for a while to greet guests, receive congratulations, and for picture-taking. When the first guests arrived at the reception hall, everything was in place: there was an outstanding band playing the music Lauren requested. No one suspected that the four-piece band with its keyboardist, two guitarists and drummer was a replacement band. The keyboardist sang lead; the others, background. Karen asked Helen how she was able to find a band so quickly, and one that played so beautifully.

"Can you believe I saw a couple of the band members playing on the Promenade in Santa Monica one evening? They're professionals. It turns out that we have a lot of local professional bands. One of the band members teaches music in a public school. They sounded so good when I heard them that evening, that I asked them for their card." Karen's eyes widened with surprise.

"Hey, you never know when you might need a musician. I found out that just because a musician is playing in a public area for free, or tips, doesn't necessarily mean he's down on his luck or is an amateur: some just like to perform in front of an audience. And, I guess, as in this case, doing so can lead to getting more work. Well, I called a few to see if they were available, and these were. Tomorrow would've been a different story though." Helen paused for a moment, took a deep breath, and then exhaled. "But we won't think about that, because it worked out. That's what's important." Karen nodded. She thanked Helen again; they shared a quick smile.

Chapter Twenty

It was Karen who tried to develop a relationship between her and Helen. She decided that since she had bonded with Danny and Brigit, she might as well do the same with Helen—or at least give it a try. They could at least be civil toward each other.

Danny and Lauren went to Oahu, Hawaii, for two weeks for their honeymoon. A week after they returned, Karen gave a dinner in their honor and invited the entire clan—including Helen. To her pleasant surprise, Helen accepted. Karen and Helen had not had any contact with each other since the wedding, and Karen hoped for the best.

During the meal, most of the conversation was about the wedding, reception and honeymoon. That went well. The wedding photographer hadn't finished the wedding album yet, but almost everyone had their own pictures of the wedding to share. Everyone, including Helen and those who had helped her with the band preparations had already seen the wedding video. Danny shared some of his and Lauren's honeymoon pictures while in Hawaii.

Lauren thanked the girls again for the gift she and Danny found in their home when they returned from their honeymoon: they had all chipped in and bought a painting similar to the one in the gallery of the two wild horses feeding near some horses in an enclosure. Though Lauren hadn't said anything, Karen had noticed Lauren's disappointment when someone purchased the large painting in the gallery, and she decided to ask the artist to paint a similar, but smaller painting for Lauren. She mentioned her plan to the others, and they insisted on chipping in, making it a gift from the girls. Lauren assured them that it was her favorite wedding gift.

After everyone had eaten dinner and dessert, the men went into the family room to watch TV. The boys went along with them; Melissa stayed in the dining room with the women. The women were getting along fine until Brigit brought up the music the band was playing at the reception, and mentioned that some of the music reminded her of the parties they went to while in high school. Helen laughed and agreed that it reminded her of the parties too.

"I wouldn't know," Karen lashed out. "I didn't go to too many parties in high school, and I certainly didn't go to any with you two." She leaped out of her chair, stood up, and pointed at Helen and Brigit. "And do you know why?" she demanded. Helen and Brigit looked at each other, dumbfounded, and didn't answer. Neither had thought about it, and frankly, they didn't know the answer. Brigit shrugged.

"I'll tell you why," Karen continued. "It was because I wasn't invited." Karen bolted over to Helen and got in her face. "You invited Brigit and eliminated me from everything. Everything!" she said, nearly screaming. Everyone looked at Helen and waited for a response. Tears welled in Helen's eyes. She tilted her head back and tried not to blink so the tears wouldn't come down, but they did. She brought her head forward and rolled her eyes at Karen. The tears flowed freely.

"Karen, we were kids; we're adults now." Helen shrugged her shoulders. "So you weren't invited. Why don't you just get over it and move on? It's in the past!" Helen didn't show either guilt or remorse, but disgust. It was obvious that she was fed up with the topic and didn't want to discuss it. But it was a hot topic for Karen—she couldn't get over it. And as long as Helen couldn't see that she had wronged her, Karen felt she couldn't move on.

"That's okay," Karen said smugly, "because I got to spend more time with dad. And you know what? I was his favorite." She pointed to herself and got in Helen's face. Helen looked at Karen square in the face and this time didn't blink.

"Oh, we are all aware that you were dad's favorite, Karen." Helen stood up. She made a sweeping motion with her arm to the group. "All of us," she said. "Now does that make you happy? Everything was about Karen. He was so proud of Karen. Karen did this, and Karen did that. Karen could do NO wrong. What about the rest of us? Didn't we matter?"

"It was all my fault," Frances blurted out. "I'm to blame. I think your father tried to give Karen more attention because you girls left her out of your activities, and well, I tried to make up for the time he was spending with her by giving you girls and Danny more of my time. I thought it would balance out, but I was wrong," she said. Frances covered her face with her hands and shook her head. "I was wrong." Karen stared at her mother, speechless. She was trying to make sense of what her mother and Helen had said.

"I was a child—a teenager," Helen yelled. Why don't you just let it go? Or are you going to hold on to it for the rest of our lives? You got dad, Karen. What more do you want?" Karen's anger vanished like mist in the air when the sun comes out. She glanced at the group. Everyone was looking at her—and waiting. She shrugged her shoulders; she didn't know what to say. What could she say? That she hadn't thought that there might be more than one side to the story—theirs? That she never considered that perhaps they might have been jealous of her because of her relationship with their father? No. She remained silent. Helen stormed out of the dining room.

"Helen . . . wait," Karen called out. Helen didn't. Karen followed her. Helen raced into the family room with the men; Karen was on her heels.

"Brad, I'm ready to go," Helen demanded.

"Why?" Brad asked, as he continued to watch TV. "We're in the middle of a game."

"I want to talk to you," Karen said to Helen. Helen refused to give her any eye contact; she kept her focus on Brad.

"We have nothing to talk about," Helen said. "Brad, let's go."

Brad turned his attention away from the TV, raised his head and focused on Helen, giving her his complete attention.

"We're not going anywhere, Helen," he said. He spoke calmly but forcefully. "You're going to talk to Karen and clear up whatever's going on between you two." He then lowered his head, faced the TV, and went back to watching it. Helen's eyes got big. She took a quick look at the other men, who were staring at her, and then she let out a sigh. She retreated, fleeing from the room; Karen followed.

Brad felt the eyes of the other men staring at him: they were dumbfounded. They were wondering if he had thought seriously about what he had done, and if he had considered possible repercussions for his action. Prior to this, they couldn't understand why this 'real man' allowed his wife to run the household and, from their perspective, him. They didn't know that Brad was the master in his home; he was a good one. And now with this action, they couldn't believe he stepped out of line and publicly reproved Helen. They stared and waited.

"What . . . ?" he asked. He shrugged his shoulders. "It's for her own good. They need to learn to get along." The men nodded in agreement, stared a couple of seconds more in disbelief, and went back to watching the game. Helen raced to the bathroom, stormed in and slammed the door behind her. Karen got up close to the door and begged Helen to open it.

"Go away!" Helen shouted. "Leave me alone!"

"Helen, please come out. I'm sorry. If you come out, I promise not to bring up the past again." Karen took a deep breath. "I'll let it go," Karen promised. Karen heard movement on the other side of the door, but Helen didn't say a word. Helen blew her nose. "Please," Karen pleaded. This was a first for Karen: people usually pleaded with her, not the other way around. But she desperately wanted Helen to respond, and she was sincerely sorry.

"Go away." Helen sniffled. "I'll come out in a few minutes. Go back with the others, and when I come back, we'll act like this never happened. There will be no further discussion. Do you understand?" Karen nodded even though Helen couldn't see her through the door.

"Okay . . . thank you," Karen said. Karen returned to the dining room, head hanging and shoulders slumped. The others stared at her, waiting for an explanation.

"Helen said she'll be out in a few minutes," Karen said. "And our, uh, little disagreement never happened. We are not to bring it up." The group looked at each other, then her, and nodded. They returned to discussing Lauren's wedding and reception.

Several minutes later, Helen entered, dabbing her swollen, pink eyes with tissue. The others continued with their conversation. Helen sat down and joined in the conversation. Other than Helen occasionally having to blow her nose, everything resumed as before. No one mentioned the blowup.

In the car, on their way home, Brad asked Helen if she and Karen had settled their differences. Helen told Brad that as far as she and Karen were concerned, it was over; they had agreed that they were not going to bring up that incident or the past again. She didn't tell him that she had no plans of dealing with Karen in the near or far future. Helen felt that her answer would be sufficient to avoid any further discussion with Brad about the subject.

Brad gave her a quick look. He wasn't quite sure what her statement meant, but he could detect that she was holding back some information. He wanted to pursue it but decided to let it go and not ask additional questions—especially in front of the boys.

* * *

The phone rang. Helen walked over to pick it up and noticed Karen's number on the display. She had reached her hand out to pick the phone up, and then snatched it back. She tucked some loose hair dangling around her face, to behind her ears. It had been less than a week since the blowup with Karen, and she wasn't in the mood to talk to her. Her anger and hurt were fresh and had not died down. She hovered over the phone, waiting for it to stop ringing.

Brad entered the room. Curious as to why Helen was standing next to the ringing phone and not answering it, he asked her if she was going to get the phone.

"I'm busy right now," she said. "I don't have time to talk to anyone."

"Is that right?" he said as he eyed the display. Brad snatched up the phone just as the answering machine's message began, and he answered it. The message stopped. Helen started to walk away. Brad raised his index finger to signal Helen to wait a minute.

Karen asked to speak to Helen. He raised an eyebrow and stared at Helen. Helen waved her hands back and forth at Brad, signaling that she didn't want to talk.

"Hold on a minute, Kar," he said. "She's right here. I'll hand her the phone." Brad held the phone out to Helen, gave her a look, daring her to refuse it, and waited for her to take the phone. She took the phone from him and rolled her eyes at him. Brad stood his ground. He crossed his arms and refused to leave while Helen was on the phone. She put the phone to her ear.

"Yes . . . ?" Helen answered.

"Hi, Helen . . . I'm having a mini luncheon next Saturday for us girls, and I'm hoping that you'll come too."

"Next Saturday?" Helen repeated. "I'm sorry, Karen, but I have other plans; Josh has a game." She was grateful she didn't have to lie and come up with an excuse: Josh really did have a game. But she did lie when she said she was sorry, because she wasn't.

"It's okay, Helen, I'll take the boys if you need to be somewhere," Brad yelled so his voice could be heard by Karen over the phone. Helen gave Brad a scowl and remained silent. Brad nodded. Helen shook her head.

"We didn't hang out together when we were coming up," Karen said, "so I was hoping that we could do it now that we're older. I really would like you to come, Helen."

Helen looked at Brad. He had gotten close enough to where he could and was breathing on her. "I'll see," Helen said. "I can't say for sure."

"She'll be there," Brad said into the phone, daring Helen to refute him. Helen sighed.

"Well . . . it looks like I'll be there," she said with no emotion. Brad smiled.

"Okay . . . then I'll see you then," Karen said. "Come between 11:30 and 12." Helen agreed. They hung up. Brad pulled Helen's head onto his chest and stroked her short hair.

"It'll be okay," he said. "You'll see . . . It'll be okay." Helen closed her eyes and sighed. She said nothing.

* * *

Helen didn't waste her time trying to get out of the lunch; Brad had made it clear that she was going and that he was sure it was going to work out. When it was time to go to the luncheon, she left, looking dejected.

When Helen arrived at Karen's, she found Brigit and Lauren happy to be there and overjoyed that she had joined them. Karen had ordered sandwiches from a local deli along with chips and soda. The girls talked about the latest movies they'd seen, Hollywood gossip, and played a couple of card games. It was difficult at first to include Helen, because she didn't want to converse.

Karen experienced first-hand how she had been in the past when attending family events. She saw how difficult she had made it for the others to warm up to her. But unlike them, she didn't give up; she was persistent. After a while, Helen warmed up and joined in with them, and they had fun. They all agreed to have "girls' night" out like the guys with their night out, and more important, Helen and Karen reconciled. They worked together at developing the relationship they never had.

Chapter Twenty-one

The sun's fingers beamed in the bedroom along the sides of the curtains, found Karen's face, and tapped on it, urging her to wake up; she wasn't ready. She rolled over to face the other side of the room. She slid her hand along the sheet to feel Jerry; he wasn't there. She opened her eyes halfway. Jerry was sitting up, staring at her.

"What?" she whispered, completely opening one eye.

"Nothing," he said. He smiled and crossed his arms.

"Then why are you staring at me?" She opened the other eye.

Jerry leaned over her and whispered in her ear, "Because I love you." His hot breath tickled her ear; she giggled. Now she was up. She raised her head and rested on her elbow.

"Jerry, what's on your mind?" she mumbled.

"I think we should move in together," he answered.

"No," she said. She flipped over and plopped her face down into the pillow, facing away from him. She and Jerry took turns staying over each other's houses. She had already told Jerry her view on living together: she was against it. Her view hadn't changed.

She knew other couples who moved in together and consolidated their belongings; when the relationship failed, they had to divide everything. Inevitably, one of them always ended up without a home. Karen didn't want herself or Jerry to end up like that. Jerry was silent. She waited a couple of minutes for him to say something, but he didn't. She turned to face him. He reached under his pillow and slid out a small jewelry box.

"Then maybe we should get married," he said. He turned the

front of the box toward her and opened it. "Karen, will you marry me?" Karen's eyes got big. There was a ring inside. The solitaire diamond ring was huge—and radiant. Jerry took the ring out of the box and reached for her hand. She gave him her outstretched, opened hand, separating her fingers. He gently slipped the ring on her finger. "Will you marry me?" he asked again. Karen sat up and admired the ring. She tilted her hand to the front, back, and side to side. The diamond sparkled; light bounced off it and winked at her. She looked at Jerry dreamy-eyed and smiled. She threw herself on him.

"Of course I'll marry you," she said, kissing him over and over again. She paused and took a breath. "Just one thing, Jerry."

"What's that?"

"I want you to ask mom before we consider it official. I think she'd like that."

"Okay, consider it done." Jerry smiled, and then feigned a worried look. "And what if she says, no?" he asked. Karen laughed.

"Are you kidding? She's probably been waiting for you to do it. If she could, she would've asked *for* you. I bet she'll insist that you call her 'mom.'" Karen held out her hand and admired the ring again. "I can't wait to tell the others," she said. She wanted to tell her siblings, but not until after Jerry first spoke to Frances, and all at one time.

Several months had passed since she and Helen had patched things up. Since then, they had grown closer and regularly kept in touch. They accepted that they weren't going to agree on everything, and that that wasn't a requirement for them to get along. They felt free to share their opinions with each other and to disagree.

"Let's do it soon," Karen insisted—"like today."

"Okay," he laughed. Karen called Frances and asked if she and Jerry could stop by for a quick visit. Frances told them they could. Shortly after they arrived at Frances' home, Karen excused herself, saying she had to go to the kitchen to get something to drink. That left Jerry and Frances alone, sitting in the living room, giving Jerry the chance to pop the question. Jerry didn't allow Frances to start a conversation on another topic. He wanted to get right to the business at hand. As soon as Karen exited, he dove in.

"Frances," Jerry began. "I think you know that I love Karen."

"Yes—you can marry her," Frances blurted out with the enthusiasm of a contest winner sure of having the right answer. She got ready to get up from the sofa and go over to Jerry to embrace him. Jerry stopped her.

"Wait," Jerry said. He held up his hands as though he were a policeman directing traffic to stop. "Let's do this right so I can say I asked you. Okay?" Jerry nodded his head slowly and waited for Frances to agree. Frances could barely contain herself. She gave him a huge smile and nodded. She settled back down on the sofa, folded her hands and placed them on her lap.

"Okay, son," she said. "Go ahead." Jerry cleared his throat and began again.

"As I was saying, I think you know I love Karen. I'm here to ask you for her hand in marriage. I want her to be my wife. May we have your blessing?" Frances clapped her hands together.

"Yes, you can marry Karen," she said. Jerry and Frances stood up, walked toward each other and embraced. Jerry breathed a sigh of relief. Karen entered the room.

"Did Jerry ask you?" Karen asked although the smiles and hug she had just witnessed answered her question.

"Yes, and I gave my blessing. I am so happy for you, Karen—for the two of you. So happy." Frances reached out and hugged Karen.

"Thanks, mom," Karen said.

"If you don't have any other plans, Frances, we'd like you to join us for lunch," Jerry said.

"I need just a few minutes to get ready," she said. Frances stroked the side of Jerry's arm. "And you can call me 'mom'; I'd like that."

"Okay, mom," Jerry said.

Karen caught Jerry's eye, gave him an "I told you so" look and winked at him. Jerry chuckled and nodded, acknowledging he understood the look.

It was going to be very difficult for Karen to keep her engagement a secret from her siblings—including Lauren, but she wanted to tell everyone at the same time. That meant she had to get the whole family together.

Frances said she would have everyone over for dinner and promised not to tell anyone about the engagement. But the dinner wouldn't be possible during the week because of work and school schedules; it had to be the weekend. That meant Karen had to wait a week—an entire week. It was killing her. She had to tell someone, and of course, that person was her best friend Ana. Karen reasoned that since Ana wasn't going to be at the family dinner, it didn't count if she told her. This information could not be shared over the phone; she had to tell Ana in person.

Immediately after she and Jerry had lunch with Frances and took her home, Karen had Jerry drive by the gallery so she could tell Ana the news in person. Jerry waited in the car while Karen went in to share the news with Ana. It was a slow day: Ana was inside, alone. Karen burst in the door, rushing onto Ana with her hand held high, showing off the ring. Ana's eyes got big. She screamed.

"Jerry asked you to marry him?" she asked. Karen nodded. Ana admired the ring and screamed again. They hugged and rocked from side to side.

"I knew it, I knew it, I knew it," Ana screamed.

"I didn't tell the others yet. And you know you're my maid of honor." Ana nodded and smiled. Ever since they were teenagers, they had promised to be each other's maid of honor; that had not changed.

"You know I helped you two get together," Ana said.

"I know," Karen said. Ana stared at Karen and waited. Karen smiled. "Okay . . . thank you, Ana. Satisfied?"

"Yes," Ana answered. Ana looked over at, and through, the gallery's glass front; she could see Jerry in the car looking at them. He waved at Ana. She waved back.

"You're going to be happy, Karen. Jerry's a really nice guy."

"I know," Karen said. "I'm already happy. We have so much in common. It's like we're made for each other. It's amazing." The girls stared at each other and nodded. "I guess I'd better go now. I'll be back a little later. We can talk some more, and I can give you all the details." Karen hugged Ana again and left.

* * *

Frances invited the entire family, including Pam and Scott over for dinner the next Saturday. The week seemed like an eternity to Karen, but it finally arrived, and they were all together. Halfway through dinner, Jerry stood up, cleared his throat to get everyone's attention, and said he wanted to make an announcement.

"You and Karen are getting married?" Helen, Brigit and Lauren asked with excitement, almost in unison. They opened their mouths, waiting for confirmation so they could scream. Frances beamed; Pam laughed. Danny and the other men looked at each other and laughed too. Scott looked around, wondering what was going on. Jerry's surprise was ruined. The smile he had tried to hide when he thought he was sharing some eye-popping news, vanished. He squinted his eyes at the group.

"How did you know? Who told you?" he asked. He examined their faces for traces of guilt. The women laughed; Scott figured out what was going on and joined in on the laughter.

"No one told us, Jerry," Helen said. "We knew it was going to happen eventually; we were hoping it would be soon."

"Let us see the ring, Karen," Brigit chimed in. The others nodded. Karen got up, walked around the table and waved her hand in front of each one to show off the ring.

"So, have you decided when you want to do this?" Brigit asked.

"We . . ."

"Not yet," Karen answered, cutting Jerry off. "I'm just getting used to being engaged. There's no need for us to rush into marriage."

Jerry snapped his head in Karen's direction, raised an eyebrow and gave her a look that made it clear that he did not agree with her statement. The others were looking at Karen, so they didn't notice Jerry's visual message to Karen. Karen shifted her eyes from Jerry to the group and refused to give him any further eye contact.

"We're going to take it slow," she said.

"Well, when you do decide, you have to get a wedding

planner," Helen insisted.

"That's right," Lauren agreed. "It'll definitely be worth it. Learn from my experience. We don't want any more near disasters in the family—one was enough." Karen smiled and nodded. She continued to avoid eye contact with Jerry.

"Even though I don't know exactly when we're getting married, I do know that I want all of you girls in my wedding. Ana's going to be my maid of honor and I'd like you all to be my bridesmaids. It'll be perfect." Karen looked over at Frances, who was smiling and nodding in approval. And the girls unanimously agreed to be her bridesmaids.

For the rest of the evening, Karen did her best to avoid eye contact with Jerry, which was pretty hard to do since he never took his eyes off her for more than a couple of seconds. After all, he did have to give some eye contact to whomever he spoke to.

From across the room, while talking to someone, he'd have his eyes on Karen. The others thought it was because he was so much in love with her, but Karen knew it was because he disagreed with her earlier statement. And Jerry had a way of sending signals with his eyes that didn't require interpretation: they were crystal clear. There was no way Karen could say she didn't understand the significance of any of Jerry's signals.

Karen tried to prolong her visit with her mother to delay the impending discussion with Jerry, but after everyone else had gone and Frances started yawning, Karen had no choice: they had to leave.

Neither Karen nor Jerry said one word to each other in the car on the way home; there was total silence. Karen reached over and turned on some music to relieve the tension and change the mood; Jerry turned it off. He gave her a quick look and continued to drive. She knew not to turn it on again. It was a long ride. West Hollywood never seemed so far from Culver City as it did that evening. They finally arrived at Karen's house. Jerry turned into the driveway and turned the car off. Before he could take the key out of the ignition, Karen broke the silence.

"Jerry, I think instead of spending the night, you should go home. If you want, we can talk tomorrow." She knew he wanted to talk. She thought that by putting it off until the next day, he may have calmed down and would possibly decide not to pursue it.

"Nooo," he said, dragging out the word and shaking his head as though he were disciplining a toddler. "I'm staying here tonight, and we'll talk in the morning." He took the key out of the ignition. That was the end of the discussion. Jerry was so good about letting Karen have her way, she knew enough to back off when he insisted on something. It meant it was important to him and she was going to lose.

When they went in the house, the two immediately started preparing for bed, neither saying a word. Once they were in the bed, Karen turned on her side in a fetal position away from Jerry. Jerry snuggled up behind her, put his arm around her and pulled her into him. He didn't say a word. Karen sighed and waited. Silence. He had said they would talk in the morning, and that was his plan; he was not going to force the issue.

"Okay," Karen said, still facing away from him. "Let's talk." Jerry raised himself up on his elbow, pressing against her.

"Do you love me?" Jerry whispered in Karen's ear. Karen wriggled her body to turn around and face him. She stared in his eyes for a long time without answering. She took a deep breath.

"Let me think about it for a minute," she said in jest. Jerry didn't smile; he didn't find it humorous.

"I'm serious, Karen." He gave her a look; it pierced through her soul. The same eyes that could make her feel warm and cozy now made her squirm and feel uncomfortable; she couldn't bear it.

"Yes, I love you. You know I do."

"Then when are we getting married?" he asked.

"Jerry, I thought maybe sometime next year." Karen had always wanted a June wedding. It was almost the middle of May, so a June wedding was out of the question unless they got married the following year.

"No, that won't work," Jerry said.

"And what would work for you, Jerry?" she asked with a sigh.

"A couple of months."

"A couple of months? I need more time than that to reserve a church and reception hall—and what about our honeymoon?

Where are we going? We have to make arrangements for that in advance too." With Jerry, silence said more than a drawn-out lecture. He didn't say a word; he just looked at her. Karen sighed again.

"Okay," Karen said, giving in. "Why don't we plan for six months? Maybe that'll work out."

"Three would be better."

"That's too soon. I can't get everything done in that short period of time."

"Try." They stared at each other. He nodded and waited for her to agree.

"Okay, I'll shoot for three, but I don't think it's realistic." Jerry shrugged his shoulders, gave her one of his smug smiles, and kissed her. He lay on his back and looked at the ceiling.

"I trust you'll do your best in finding a date we can both agree on." He looked over at Karen. She nodded but thought about the almost impossible task she had before her of trying to pull everything together for a wedding in such a short period of time. She put her head on Jerry's chest, closed her eyes and fell asleep.

Once Jerry and Karen agreed to get married within a few months, time passed by rapidly. Before any arrangements were made, Karen hired a wedding planner. Finding a church was easier than finding a reception hall: most were booked through the end of the year. Karen wasn't able to find one available within the three-month time frame Jerry had asked for, but she found one available in five months—in October—close enough for Jerry to live with. It also gave Karen extra time to take care of all the other arrangements.

She and Jerry decided to go to Italy for their honeymoon. Jerry had traveled there before, but he was looking forward to viewing artworks in Italy's museums and cathedrals with his new bride. And for Karen, it was a honeymoon location she often dreamed of that soon was to become a reality. They both looked forward to it—perhaps more than the actual wedding.

Karen asked for input from her mom, siblings and Ana to assist her with the wedding plans. Together, they made the decisions, and the wedding planner made them happen. Money was not a problem. Jerry was footing the entire bill, and he wanted everything to be exactly as Karen wanted. For many years, Karen thought of herself as Cinderella, with a wicked stepmother and two evil stepsisters. Now, she took on the role of someone she could not remember reading about in the children's stories: that of one of three princesses, of a kind queen, who was about to marry her Prince Charming. Life was good; Karen was happy.

When the time came for the wedding, there was no doubt it would go smoothly, and it did. Karen asked Danny to give her away, and he joked about how much joy he was going to get from doing that. Having the reception hall decorated with a Monet-type theme and then following that with going to Venice, Rome and Florence, Italy, on her honeymoon was for Karen a dream come true.

Chapter Twenty-two

Karen continued her weekly mom-time with Frances, and the family agreed to get together once a month as a group. This continued for four years. They became a very close-knit family. During that time, Danny and Lauren became the proud parents of a beautiful baby boy. Jerry and Karen decided to wait a while before having offspring. They enjoyed doing things together as a couple.

Frances's 70th birthday was coming up. The Andersen siblings decided to throw a big bash for her birthday, and to make it a combination birthday party/family reunion.

Helen was handling most of the arrangements—that had not changed with time. She and Karen had been going back and forth with the menu for the party. Jerry and Karen were in the middle of eating dinner in a restaurant when Helen called Karen on her cell phone. Karen glanced at her phone and saw that it was Helen.

"It's Helen," she said to Jerry. "I'll tell her I'll call her back." She answered the phone. "Hey, Helen, Jerry and I are out to dinner. Can it wait? I'll call you later?" Silence. "Helen . . ?"

"No, it can't wait, Karen," Helen said, her voice trembling.

"Mom had a heart attack; it's pretty bad. The doctors don't think she's going to make it through the night. You should come right away." Karen nodded but said nothing. Tears welled in her eyes and then streamed down her face. Her throat tightened; she could not speak.

"Karen . . . Karen, did you hear me?" Helen yelled in the phone. Karen pulled the phone from her ear and looked at it.

"Karen? Karen, are you there?" Jerry could hear Helen

frantically calling out. He took the phone out of Karen's hand and held it to his ear.

"Helen . . . what's wrong?" he asked. Helen gave him the news.

"Where is she?" he asked. Helen gave him the information. "We'll be there as fast as we can," he said. Jerry hung up. Karen sat frozen.

"Karen, we've got to leave now. We're going to the hospital to see mom," he said in a voice just above a whisper. Karen nodded but didn't say a word. He signaled the waiter to bring the check. "She'll be okay," Jerry kept saying. "She's a strong woman." Karen nodded in agreement, but her eyes showed signs of fear and despair. Jerry paid the check, helped Karen to her feet, and they left the restaurant.

When Jerry and Karen arrived at the hospital, Frances was surrounded by Brigit, Helen, Danny, Lauren and Pam. Brad and Michael were standing in the background. Helen was stroking Frances' hair while Pam was holding one of her hands. Karen rushed to the bed and grabbed Frances' free hand, stroking it. Jerry made his way through, leaned over Frances and kissed her forehead.

"It's me, Jerry, mom. Karen and I are here. We're here with the others. We're staying until you get better," he whispered. "We're not going anywhere." He then left the area and joined Brad and Michael. Frances' eyes were half closed. She opened them as best she could. She looked completely exhausted. She struggled to talk; her mouth quivered, but nothing came out.

"Mom, please don't die. Don't leave me. You can't die," Karen begged. Karen started sobbing.

"Karen?" Frances whispered.

"Yes?" Karen said, as she quieted down so she could hear Frances speak. She put her ear close to Frances' mouth.

"Yes, mom?"

"I can't always be with you; you know that. I'm ready to go. I'm ready to go with your father. You children have each other to look out for, and well . . . you and I, we've made peace." Karen raised her head and stared at Frances in disbelief.

"We made peace?" Karen repeated. "And so now you can

leave me? I don't understand." Karen looked at her siblings for an explanation—for clarification. They offered none. She then turned her attention back to Frances.

"Mommy, please don't go. Our kids will never know their grandmother. They'll never know you." Frances looked sadly into Karen's eyes.

"I'm sorry, dear," Frances said. "I can't." She then scanned the group, moving only her eyes. "I love all of you, and I know you all love me too. I'm happy . . . and I'm not afraid to go; I'm ready to go." She gave a little nod. "I want to go," she said. Frances then took a quick breath, smiled, and passed away. Karen put her head on her mother's chest and sobbed. The others, while struggling with their own loss, tried to console Karen in hers.

Made in the USA
Middletown, DE
06 October 2023

40310983R00080